'I don't understand,' she whispered. She was near tears again. She swallowed hard to stop them. Crying was the lowest type of female trick. She would not give in to it with Sam, no matter how much she hurt. 'If you love me...'

'It is not love,' he said with finality, cold and professional again. 'I doubt I am even capable of the feeling. Marry St Aldric. Be safe and happy. But for God's sake, woman, go away and leave me in peace.'

He stood and grabbed her, but it was not for another kiss. Instead he hauled her up off the floor and spun her away from him. Then he opened the door and pushed her through it and out into the hall.

The oak panel slammed behind her.

Sam looked wildly around the room, searching for the bottle that he had already packed. Rum. Stinging, harsh, and nothing like her kiss.

Nothing he had seen in his studies at land or at sea could explain the feelings coursing through him now. None of it explained the demon that possessed him, that made him want the one woman he could not have.

Don't miss this sensational new Regency duet from Christine Merrill

THE SINNER AND THE SAINT

Brothers separated at birth, brought together by scandal

From the birth of a secret to the death of a lie, two brothers have been torn apart. While the Duke behaves like a saint, the doctor believes himself a sinner. And only a scandal can bring them back together.

THE GREATEST OF SINS
May 2013

Look for the second in the duet
Coming soon

THE GREATEST OF SINS

Christine Merrill

All the characters in this book have no existence outside the imagination of the author, and have no relation whatsoever to anyone bearing the same name or names. They are not even distantly inspired by any individual known or unknown to the author, and all the incidents are pure invention.

First published in Great Britain 2013
by Mills & Boon, an imprint of Harlequin (UK) Limited.
Large Print edition 2013
Harlequin (UK) Limited, Eton House, 18-24 Paradise Road,
Richmond, Surrey TW9 1SR

ISBN: 978 0 263 23279 0

Harlequin (UK) policy is to use papers that are natural, renewable and recyclable products and made from wood grown in sustainable forests. The logging and manufacturing process conform to the legal environmental regulations of the country of origin.

Printed and bound in Great Britain
by CPI Antony Rowe, Chippenham, Wiltshire

Christine Merrill lives on a farm in Wisconsin, USA, with her husband, two sons, and too many pets—all of whom would like her to get off the computer so they can check their e-mail. She has worked by turns in theatre costuming, where she was paid to play with period ballgowns, and as a librarian, where she spent the day surrounded by books. Writing historical romance combines her love of good stories and fancy dress with her ability to stare out of the window and make stuff up.

Previous novels by Christine Merrill:

THE INCONVENIENT DUCHESS
AN UNLADYLIKE OFFER
A WICKED LIAISON
MISS WINTHORPE'S ELOPEMENT
THE MISTLETOE WAGER
(part of *A Yuletide Invitation*)
DANGEROUS LORD, INNOCENT GOVERNESS
PAYING THE VIRGIN'S PRICE*
TAKEN BY THE WICKED RAKE*
MASTER OF PENLOWEN
(part of *Halloween Temptations*)
LADY FOLBROKE'S DELICIOUS DECEPTION†
LADY DRUSILLA'S ROAD TO RUIN†
LADY PRISCILLA'S SHAMEFUL SECRET†
A REGENCY CHRISTMAS CAROL
(part of *One Snowy Regency Christmas*)
TWO WRONGS MAKE A MARRIAGE

**Regency Silk & Scandal* mini-series
†*Ladies in Disgrace* trilogy

And in Mills & Boon® Historical *Undone!* eBooks:

SEDUCING A STRANGER
TAMING HER GYPSY LOVER
VIRGIN UNWRAPPED
TO UNDO A LADY

Did you know that some of these novels are also available as eBooks? Visit www.millsandboon.co.uk

AUTHOR NOTE

To give my hero Sam Hastings a chance to use a stethoscope I had to set this story after the Napoleonic war and hope that he might have picked one up from a French ship while serving in the navy. In England, such a thing would have been unheard of, and Sam's would have been quite a novelty. While the one I give to Sam is a wooden tube, the very first one was nothing more than a rolled up piece of paper.

Rene Theophile Laënnec was the French physician who discovered that it was possible to listen to the heart through a tube. Before him, doctors would either place their ears directly on the patient's chest or pound their backs with a hammer and listen to the resonance. In 1816 poor Rene was called to treat a buxom young lady with a heart condition. He was too embarrassed to place his ear directly on her chest, and improvised a paper tube to listen through.

And thus one of the most commonplace pieces of medical equipment was invented.

DEDICATION

To James: who is living in interesting times.

Chapter One

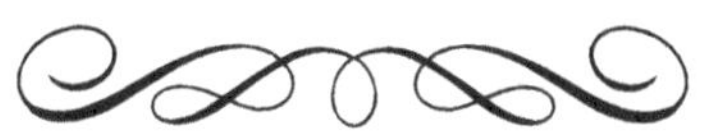

Sam was coming home!

They were such simple words to have such an effect upon her. Evelyn Thorne put a hand over her heart, feeling the frenzied beat of it at the thought of his name. How long had she been waiting for his return? Very nearly six years. He had gone off to Edinburgh when she was still in the schoolroom and she had been planning for this day ever since.

She had been sure that, following his education, he would come back for her. Some day, she would hear his light, running step on the boards of the front hallway. He would shout a welcome to Jenks, the butler, and make a joyful enquiry about her father. There would be an answering welcome call from the office at the head of the stairs, for certainly Father would be as eager to hear what his ward had made of himself as she was.

After the greetings were done with, things would return to the way they had been. They would sit in the parlor together and in the garden. She would force him to accompany her to balls and routs, which would all be less tedious with Sam there to talk to, to dance with and to protect from the marital ambitions of other girls.

At the end of the Season, he would return with them to the country. There, they would walk in the orchard and run down the path to the little pond to watch the birds and animals, lying on the rugs that he would carry, eating a picnic from a basket that she would pack with her own hands, not trusting the cook to reserve the choicest morsels for a man who was not 'truly a Thorne'.

As if to reinforce the thought, Mrs Abbott cleared her throat, from the doorway behind her. 'Lady Evelyn, would you not be more comfortable in the morning room? There is a chill in the hall. If there are guests…'

'It would be more seemly to be found there?' Eve completed with a sigh.

'If his Grace were to come...'

'But he is not the one expected, Abbott, as you know full well.'

The housekeeper gave a slight sniff of disapproval.

Evelyn turned to her, putting aside her girlish excitement. Though only one and twenty, she was mistress of the house and would be obeyed. 'I will hear none of that, from you or any other member of the staff. Doctor Hastings is as much a member of the family as I am. Perhaps more so. Father took him from the foundling home a full three years before I was even born. He has been a part of this house since my first memory and is the only brother I shall ever have.'

Of course, it had been quite some time since she had considered Sam her brother. Without thinking, she touched her lips.

Abbott's eyes narrowed slightly as she noticed the gesture.

For a moment, Eve considered making a diplomatic retreat to a receiving room. Her behaviour would be less obvious to the servants. But what message would it send to Sam if she made him come to her like an ordinary guest?

She bowed her head, as though she had considered the wisdom of Abbott's suggestion and said, 'You are right. There is a draught. If you could but bring me a shawl, I will be fine. And I shall not pace about before the window, for it will be much more comfortable on the bench beneath the stairs.' From there, she could see the front door quite well, yet be invisible to the one who entered. Her appearance would be sudden and a pleasant surprise.

As she passed it, she glanced in the hallway mirror, straightening her hair and gown, smoothing curls and fluffing ruffles. Would Sam find her pretty, now that she had grown? The Duke of St Aldric had proclaimed her the handsomest girl at Almack's and a diamond of the first water. But he was so easy in his compliments that she quite wondered if he was sincere. His manners would have required him to say such, once he had set his sights upon her.

In the same situation, Sam would have offered

no false flattery. He might have pronounced her attractive. If she had begged for more, wishing to be called beautiful, he would have accused her of vanity and named several girls that he found prettier.

Then he would have eased the sting by reminding her that she was fair enough for the average man. He would say that, for a humble man like himself, she was like a vision from heaven. Then he would smile at her, to prove that they understood each other. And his comment would make all other suitors seem unworthy.

But he'd had no chance to make such observations, because he had not come back for her first Season. He had gone straight from university, into the navy. It had been several years since. She had spent it scouring the papers for news of his ship and taking care to become the sort of woman he might hope to find when he returned. She had crossed days off the calendar and told herself each December that, next year, the wait would be over. He would come home and she would be ready for him.

But the only contact from Sam was a terse letter to Father that had outlined his plans to take a position on the *Matilda*.

And he had written not a word to her since the day he had left. She had not even heard of his appointment as a ship's surgeon until after he had set sail. There had been no chance to reason him into a safer plan. He was gone and that was that.

Three years of dragging her feet had kept her in the marriage mart. She could not possibly make a match until she had seen him again. People thought it quite odd that she had not accepted an offer already. If she refused St Aldric, she would be properly on the shelf, too high in the instep for any man. Any save one, of course.

The knock came at the door, sharp and sudden, and she started in her chair. It had not sounded the way she'd imagined it would. Although how much personality could be conveyed with a door knocker, she was not sure. All the same, it startled her.

Instead of rushing forwards to open it for him, she drew back into the little space beneath the curve of the stairs. It was cowardly of her. But the secrecy meant that she would catch the first glimpse of him without his knowing and keep the moment all to herself. She would not need to guard her expression from the servants. She could devour the sight of him, thinking of things that had nothing to do with walks in the garden and picnics by the stream.

Jenks came forwards and opened the door, his tall, straight body hiding the man on the steps. The request for entrance was firm and had a polite warmth, but it was not as impulsive or raucous as she had imagined. She had been thinking of the boy who had left, she reminded herself, not the man he had become. He would still be Sam, of course. But he was changed, just as she was.

The person who appeared in the doorway was a strange combination of novelty and familiarity. He walked with the upright gait of a military man, but was free of the scars and disabilities she had seen in so many returning officers. Of course, he had spent his time well away from the battle proper, below decks, tending to the injuries that resulted from it.

He was still blond, although the reddish highlights in his hair had gone dark, almost brown.

The boyish softness had left his cheeks, replaced by a firm jaw line scraped clean of stubble. His eyes were still blue, of course, and as sharp and inquisitive as ever. They took in the hall at a glance, looking at it much the same as she was looking at him, noting changes and similarities. He completed the survey with a brief nod before enquiring if her father was at home to visitors.

The boy she remembered had had a sunny disposition, an easy smile and a hand always reaching out to help or to comfort, but the man who stood before her now, in a navy-blue coat, was sombre. One might call him grave. She supposed it was a necessity of his profession. One did not want a doctor delivering bad news with a smile upon his face. But it was more than that. Though his eyes held great compassion, they were bleak, as though he suffered along with the suffering.

She wanted to ask if his life in the navy had been as horrible as she'd imagined. Had it troubled him to see so many mangled bodies and to do so little for them? Were the successes he had won from death enough to compensate for the brutality of war? Had it really changed him so much? Or did anything remain of the boy who had left her?

Now that he was back, she wanted to ask so many things. Where had he been? What had he done there? And, most importantly, why had he left her? She had thought, as they had grown past the age of playmates, that they were likely to become something much more.

His current disposition, as he passed her hiding place and followed Jenks up the stairs, was a stark contrast to St Aldric, who always seemed to be smiling. Though the duke had many responsibilities, his face was not as careworn, or marked, as Sam's. He greeted obstacles with optimism. But he had a right to do so. There seemed little that he could not accomplish.

In looks, she could see many similarities between the two men. Both were fair and blue eyed. But St Aldric was the taller of the two and the handsomer as well. In all things physical, he was the superior. He had more power, more money, rank and title.

And yet he was not Sam. She sighed. No amount of common sense would sway her heart from its choice. If she accepted the inevitable offer, she would be quite happy with St Aldric, but she would never love him.

But if the person one truly loved above all others was not interested, what was one to do?

Just now, he had gone straight to her father, without enquiring of Lady Evelyn's location. Perhaps he did not care. In his silent absence, Samuel Hastings seemed to be saying that he did not remember her in the same way she did him. Perhaps he still thought of her as a childhood friend and not a young lady of marriageable age who might have formed an attachment to him.

Did he not remember the kiss? When it had happened, she had been sure of her feelings.

Apparently, he had not. After, he'd grown cold and distant. She could not believe that he was the sort of youth who would steal a kiss just to prove that he could. Had she done something to offend? Perhaps she had been too eager. Or not enthusiastic enough. But how could he have expected her to know what to do? It had been her first kiss.

It had changed everything between them. Overnight, his smile had disappeared. And, shortly thereafter, he had been gone in body as well as spirit.

Even if she had misunderstood, she would have thought that he might have written a note of farewell. Or he could have answered at least one of the letters she'd sent to him, dutifully, every week. Perhaps he had not received them. On one of his brief visits home from school, she had enquired of them. He had admitted, with a curt nod and a frozen smile, that he had read them. But he'd added nothing to indicate that the messages provided any comfort or pleasure.

It was a moot point now, of course. When one had captured the attention of a duke, who was not only powerful and rich, but handsome, polite and charming, one should not lament over a snub from a physician of no real birth.

She sighed again. All the same, it had been much on her mind of late. Even if he did not love her, Sam had been her friend. Her dearest, closest companion. She wanted his opinion of St Aldric: of the man, and of her decision. If there was any reason that he disapproved...

Of course, there could not be. He would bring no last-minute reprieve with an offer of his own. And she must remind herself that it was not exactly a march to the gallows, becoming Her Grace, the Duchess of St Aldric.

But if he did not want her, the least Dr Samuel Hastings could do was give his congratulations. And that might make it possible for her to move forwards.

'A ship's surgeon.' Lord Thorne's tone was flat with disapproval. 'Is that not a job that can be done by a carpenter? Surely a university-trained physician could have done better.'

Sam Hastings faced his benefactor's dark look with military posture and an emotionless stare. He could remember a time when his actions had met with nothing but approval from this man. In response, Sam had been eager to please and desperately afraid of disappointing him. But it seemed that his best efforts to abide by Thorne's final instructions to 'make something of yourself' were to be met with argument and doubt.

So be it. His need to prove himself had cooled

when Thorne's affection had. 'On the contrary, sir. On most ships, they are forced by a scarcity of skill to make do with any willing man. While they often employ the carpenter's mate for the job, no one wants to be the man's first patient. I am sure both captain and crew appreciated my help. I saved more limbs than I took. I gained experience with many diseases that I might never have seen had I remained ashore. There were some tropical fevers that were quite challenging. The time not spent in action was spent in study. There are many hours in the normal running of the ship that can be devoted to education.'

'Hmmmpf.' His guardian's foul mood turned to resignation, when presented with reasonable opposition. 'If you could find no other way to get sufficient experience, then I suppose it had to do.'

'And it was quite far away,' Sam added, subtly colouring the words. 'When I left, you encouraged me to travel.'

'That is true.' Now Thorne was circumspect, which might be as close as Sam could get to approval. 'And you have made no plans towards marriage? I encouraged you to that as well.'

'Not as yet, sir. There was little opportunity, when so totally in the company of men. But I have ample prize money in the bank and a plan to set up practice.'

'In London?' Thorne said, brows furrowing.

'In the north,' Sam assured him. 'I can certainly afford wife and family. I am sure there will be some woman not averse…' He left the ending open, not wanting to lie outright. Let Thorne think what he liked. There would be no marriage, no children, no future of that sort at all.

'Evelyn, of course, is on the cusp of a great match,' Thorne said, as though relieved to change the subject. He smiled with obvious pride of his only daughter. For Sam's sake, the words were delivered with an air of finality.

Sam nodded. 'So I was given to understand by your letters. She is to marry a duke?'

Now, Thorne was beaming with satisfaction. 'Despite his rank, St Aldric is the most magnanimous of gentlemen. He is so full of good humour and generosity that his friends have shortened the title to Saint.'

Evie had won herself a saint, had she? It was

no less than she deserved. Sam had best keep as far away from her as possible. His own nature proved him to be as far from that lofty state as it was possible to be. 'Evelyn is the most fortunate of young ladies to gain such a husband.'

'It is a shame that you cannot stay to meet him. He is expected this afternoon.' It was as blunt as shutting the door in his face. Being 'like a member of the family' was not the same as recognised kinship. Now that he was raised and settled in a trade, Thorne felt no responsibility to him at all.

'A pity, indeed. But, of course, I cannot stay,' Sam agreed. It was just as well. He had no real desire to meet this Saint who would marry his Evie, or remain under the Thorne roof a moment more than was necessary. 'You will give my regards to Lady Evelyn, of course.' He added her title carefully, to avoid any sign of familiarity.

'Of course,' her father said. 'And now, I do not wish to keep you.'

'Of course not.' Sam managed a smile and rose, as though this brief visit had been his intent all along, and his departure had nothing to do with the abrupt dismissal. 'I only wished to thank you, sir, and to remind you of the difference your patronage has meant to my life. A letter hardly seemed appropriate.' Sam offered a stiff bow to the man who had claimed to be his benefactor.

Thorne got up from his desk and clapped him by the shoulder, smiling as he had of old. That such approval could only come by his leaving was another bitter reminder of how things had changed. 'I am touched, my boy. And it is good to know that you are doing well. Will we see you, again, while you are in London? For the wedding, perhaps?' When it was too late for him to do any harm.

'I do not know. My plans are not yet set.' If he could find a ship in need of his services, he would be gone with the tide. And if not? Perhaps there was some distant spot in Scotland or Ireland that had need of a physician.

'You are welcome, of course. We will have much to celebrate. Little Eve is not so little any more. St Aldric has been quite set on the match, since the beginning of the Season, but she has yet to answer him. I have told her that it does not do to play with the affections of a duke. She will not listen.' Thorne still smiled, as though even her disobedience was a treasure, which of course, to him, it was.

If he had continued to indulge her every whim, she had likely grown into a wilful hoyden. She would run wild without a strong man to partner her. Himself, for instance… Sam put the thought from his head. 'She will come round in time, I am sure, sir.' With luck, he would be gone without seeing it happen. If she had not decided, it would be disaster to hang about here and run the risk of muddying her mind with his presence.

He and Thorne went through the motions of an amicable parting as he walked towards the door of the room, but it went no further than that. They might as well have been strangers, for all the emotion expressed. There had been a time when Sam had longed for a deeper bond of affection. But now that he knew the truth of their relationship, he would as soon have never met the man. It took only a few more empty promises to keep in contact, before the interview was at an end and he was out of the office and retreating down the main stairs of the house he had once thought his home.

Only a few more feet and he would be out the front door and away. But a departure without incident was unlikely, since, as he had climbed the stairs to Thorne's office, he had known that *she* waited, scant feet away.

When he had passed through on the hallway, he had taken great care not to look too closely at the place she must be concealed. He did not want to see her. It would make leaving all the more difficult.

But as he'd approached the house, a part of him had feared that she would not be there to greet him. That poor fool had wanted to search the corners for her, to hold out his arms and call out her name. He would be equally foolish to suffer if she did not come to him, or if she had already gone into the arms and the house of another. One could not bring back the past, especially when one found that the happiness there had been based on ignorance and illusion.

The door had opened and he had not seen her. Torn between fear and relief, he had been afraid to enquire after her. But then, as he had passed her hiding place, he had smelled her perfume.

That was not wholly accurate. He could smell a woman's scent in the air of the hall, fresh and growing stronger as he neared the alcove at the curve of the stairs. He could not be sure it was her. The girl he had left had smelled of lemon soap and the mildest lavender eau de toilette. This new perfume was redolent of India, mysterious, sharp and sophisticated.

He should have simply turned and acknowledged her. He'd have caught her hiding at the base of the stairs, for he was sure that was what she had been doing, just as she had done when they were children. He could have pretended that nothing was amiss and greeted her easily, as an old friend ought. They could have exchanged pleasantries. Then he could have wished her well and they'd have parted again after a few words.

But the fragrance had been an intoxicant to him and he would have needed all his wits for even a few words of greeting. If he could not master himself, there was no telling what his first words would have been. So he had taken the coward's way, pretending that he was unaware of her presence and hoping that she would have given up in the hour of the interview and gone back to the morning room, or wherever it was that she spent her days.

He could not imagine his Evie, sitting like a lady on a divan or at a writing desk, prepared to offer a gracious but chilly welcome and banal conversation. He had spent too many years brooding on the memory of how she had been, not wanting her to change. He could picture her in the garden, running, climbing and sitting on the low tree branches he had helped her to, when no one had been there to stop them.

Yet she would have put that behaviour aside, just as she had the eau de toilet. She had grown up. She was to be a duchess. The girl he remembered was gone, replaced by a *ton*-weary flirt with poise enough to keep a duke dangling. Once he had met that stranger, perhaps he could finally be free of her and have some peace.

Then, as he reached the bottom step, she pelted out from hiding and into him, body to body, her arms around his neck, and called, 'Tag.' Her lips were on his cheeks, first one, then the other, in a pair of sisterly but forceful kisses.

He froze, body and mind stunned to immobility. With preparation, he had controlled his first reaction to her nearness. But this sudden and complete contact was simply too much. His arms had come halfway up to hug her before he'd managed to stop them and now they poked stiffly out at the elbows, afraid to touch her, unable to show any answering response. 'Evie,' he managed in a tone as stiff as his posture. 'Have you learned no decorum at all in six years?'

'Not a whit, Sam,' she said, with a laugh. 'You did not think to escape me so easily, did you?'

'Of course not.' Hadn't he tried, going nearly to the ends of the earth to do so? If that had been a failure, what was he to do now? 'I'd have greeted you properly, had you given me the chance,' he lied. He reached up and pried her arms from his neck, stepping away from her.

She gave him a dour frown, meant to be an imitation of his own expression, he was sure. Then she laughed again. 'Because we must always be proper, mustn't we, Dr Hastings?'

He took another step back to dodge the second embrace that he knew was coming, taking her hands to avoid the feeling of her body wriggling eagerly against his. 'We are no longer children, Evelyn.'

'I should hope not.' She gave him a look that proved she was quite aware that she, at least, had grown into a desirable young woman. 'I have been out for three Seasons.'

'And kept half the men in London dangling from your reticule strings, I don't doubt.' Lud, but she was pretty enough to do it. Hair as straight and smooth as spun gold, eyes as blue as the first flowers of spring and lips that made his mouth water to taste them. And he might have known the contours of her body, had he taken the opportunity to touch it as she'd kissed him.

The thought nearly brought him to his knees.

She shrugged as if it did not matter to her what other men thought and gave him the sort of look, with lowered lashes and slanted eyes, that told a man that the woman before him cared only about him. 'And what is your diagnosis, Doctor, now that you have had a chance to examine me?'

'You look well,' he said, cursing the inadequacy of the words.

She pouted and the temptress dissolved into his old friend, swinging her arms as though inviting him to play. 'If that is all I shall have out of you, I am most disappointed, sir. I have been told by other men that I am quite the prettiest girl of the Season.'

'And that is why St Aldric has offered for you,' he said, reminding them both of how much had changed.

She frowned, but did not let go of his hands. 'As yet, I have not accepted any offers.'

'Your father told me that, just now. He said you are keeping the poor fellow on tenterhooks waiting for an answer. It is most unfair of you, Evelyn.'

'It is most unfair of Father to pressure me on the subject,' she replied, avoiding the issue. 'And even worse, it is unscientific of you to express an opinion based on so little evidence.' She smiled again. 'I would much rather you tell me what you think of my marrying, after wc have had some time together.'

'I stand by my earlier conclusion,' he said. It made him sound like one of those pompous asses who would rather stick to a bad diagnosis than admit the possibility of error. 'Congratulations are in order. Your father says St Aldric is a fine man and I have no reason to doubt it.'

She gave him a dark, rather vague look, and then smiled. 'How nice to know that you and my father are in agreement on the subject of my future happiness. Since you are dead set in seeing me married, I assume you have come prepared?'

He had fallen into a trap of some kind, he was sure. And here was one more proof that this was not the transparent child he had left, who could not keep a secret. Before him was a woman, clearly angry at his misstep, but unwilling to tell him what he had said, or how he was to make amends. 'Prepared?' he said, cautiously, looking for some hint in her reaction.

'To celebrate my imminent engagement,' she finished, still waiting. She then gave an exasperated sigh to show him that he was hopeless. 'By giving me some token to commemorate the event.'

'A gift?' Her audacity startled a smile from him and a momentary loss of control.

'My gift,' she said, firmly. 'You cannot have been away so long, missed birthdays and Christmases and a possible engagement, and brought me nothing. Must I search your pockets to find it?'

He thought of her hands, moving familiarly over his body, and said hurriedly, 'Of course not. I have it here, of course.'

He had nothing. There had been the gold chain that he'd bought for her in Minorca and then could not raise the nerve to send. He had carried it about in his pocket for a year, imagining the way it would look against the skin of her throat. Then he'd realised that it was only making the memories more vivid, more graphic, and had thrown it into the bay.

'Well?' She had noticed his moment of confusion and was tugging upon his lapel, an eager child again.

He thrust a hand into his pocket and brought out the first thing hc found, an inlaid wood case that held a small brass spyglass. 'This. I had it with me, very nearly the whole time. At sea they are dead useful. I thought, perhaps, you could use it in the country. Watching birds.'

Any other woman in London would have thrust the thing back at him in disgust, pointing out that he had not even taken the time to polish the barrel.

But not his Evie. When she opened the box, her face lit as though he had handed her a casket of jewels. Then she pulled out the glass, gave it a hurried wipe against her skirt to shine it and extended it and put it to her eye. 'Oh, Sam. It is wonderful.' She pulled him to the nearest window and peered out through it, looking as she always had, into the distance, as though she could see the future. 'The people on the other side of the square are as clear as if I was standing beside them.' She took it away from her face and grinned at him. The expression was so like the way he remembered her that his heart hurt. She was standing beside him again, so close that an accidental touch was inevitable. He withdrew quickly, ignoring the flood of memories that her nearness brought.

She seemed unmoved by his discomfort, sighing in pleasure at her improved vision. 'I will take it to the country, of course. And to Hyde Park and the opera.'

He laughed. 'If you actually need a glass in town, I will buy you a lorgnette. With such a monstrous thing pressed to your eye, you will look like a privateer.'

She let out a derisive puff of air. 'What do I care what people think? It will be so much easier to see the stage.' She gave a sly grin. 'And I will be able to spy on the other members of the audience. That is the real reason we all go to the theatre. Nothing in London shall escape me. I share the gossip the next day and show them my telescope. In a week, all the smart girls will have them.'

'Wicked creature.' Without thinking, he reached up and tugged on one honey-coloured lock. She had not changed a bit in his absence, still fresh faced, curious and so alive that he could feel her vitality coursing in the air around them.

'Let us go and watch something.' She took his hand, her fingers twining with his, pulling him back into the house and towards the doors that led to the garden that had been their haven.

And he was lost.

Chapter Two

He ought to have known better. Before coming, Sam had steeled himself against temptation with prayer. His plan had been to resist all contact with her. Just moments before, he had assured her father that he would be gone. And yet, at the first touch of her hand, he had forgotten it all and followed her through the house like a puppy on a lead.

Now he sat at her side on a little stone bench under the elm as she experimented with her new toy. It was just like hundreds of other happy afternoons spent here and it reminded him of how much he missed home, and how much a part of that home she was.

Evie held the spyglass firmly pointed into the nearest tree. 'There is a nest. And three young ones all open mouthed and waiting to be fed. Oh, Sam, it is wonderful.'

It was indeed. He could see the flush of pleasure on her cheek and the way it curved down into the familiar dimple of her smile. So excited, and over such a small thing as a nest of birds. But had she not always been just so? Joy personified and a tonic to a weary soul.

'You can adjust it, just by turning here.' He reached out and, for a moment, his hand covered hers. The shock of connection was as strong as ever. It made him wonder—did she still feel it as well? If so, she was as good at dissembling as he, for she gave no response.

'That is ever so much better. I can make out individual feathers.' She looked away from the birds, smiling at him, full of mischief. 'I clearly made the best bargain out of your empty pockets today, sir.'

'I beg your pardon?'

'If you had reached in and pulled out a snuff box, I'd have had a hard time developing the habit of taking it. But a telescope is very much to my liking.'

'Was it so obvious that I did not bring you anything?' he asked, sighing.

'The look of alarm on your face was profound,' she admitted and snapped the little cylinder shut to put it back into its case. 'But do not think that you can get this away from me by distracting me with a necklace. It is mine now and I shan't return it.'

'Nor would I expect you to.' He smiled back at her and felt the easy familiarity washing over him in a comfortable silence. With six years, thousands of miles travelled and both of them grown, none of the important things had changed between them. She was still his soul's mate. At least he could claim it was more than lust that he felt for her.

She broke the silence. 'Tell me about your travels.'

'There is not enough time to tell you all the things I have seen,' he said. But now that she had asked, the temptation to try was great and the words rushed out of him. 'Birds and plants that are nothing like you find in England. And the look of the ocean, wild or becalmed, or the sky before a storm, when there is no land in sight? The best word I can find for it is majesty. Sea and heaven stretching as far as the eye can see in all directions and us just a spot in the middle.'

'I should very much like to see that,' she said wistfully.

He imagined her, at his side, lying on the deck to look at the stars. And then he put the dream carefully away. 'Wonderful though some times were, I would not have wished them on you if it meant you saw the rest. A ship of the line is no place for a woman.'

'Was naval life really so harsh?'

'During battle, there was much for me to do,' he admitted evasively, not wanting to share the worst of it.

'But you helped the men,' she said, her face shining when she said it, as though there was something heroic about simply doing his job. 'And that was what you always wanted to do. I am sure it was most gratifying.'

'True,' he agreed. He had felt useful. And it had been a relief to find a place where he seemed to fit, after so much doubt.

'If it made you happy, then I should like to have seen that as well,' she said firmly.

'Most certainly not!' He did not want to think of her, mixed in with the blood and death. Nor did he want to lose her admiration, when she saw him helpless in the face of things that had no cure.

She gave him a pained look. 'Have you forgotten so much? Was it not I who encouraged you in your medical studies? I watched you tend every injured animal you found and dissect the failures. I swear, you did not so much eat in those days as study the anatomy of the chops.'

'I could just as easily have become butcher, for all I learned there,' he admitted. 'But working over a person is quite a different thing.' Sometimes, it was its own form of butchery.

'You learned human anatomy in Edinburgh,' she said. 'Through dissection.'

He suppressed a smile and nodded. Evie was as fearless as she had always been, and no less grisly, despite her refined appearance.

'You did many other things as well, I'm sure.'

'I observed,' he corrected. 'It was not until I

left school that I could put the skills to use. Now I am thinking of returning to Scotland,' he said, to remind them both that he could not stay. 'I still have many friends at the university. Perhaps I might lecture.'

She shook her head. 'That is too far away.'

That was why he had suggested it. She was clinging to his sleeve again, as though she could not bear to have him taken from her. He considered detaching her fingers, but it was very near to having her touch his hand, so he left them remain as they were. 'You will be far too busy with your new life to waste time upon me. I doubt you will miss me at all.'

'You know that is not true. Did I not write you often in the last years? Nearly every week, yet you never answered.' Her voice grew quiet and, in it, he could hear the hurt he had caused her.

'Probably because I did not receive your letters,' he said, as though it had not mattered to him. 'The mail is a precarious thing, when one is at sea.' He had received it often enough. And he had cherished it. In the years they'd been apart, her correspondence had grown from a neat ribbon-bound stack to a small chest, packed tightly with well-thumbed missives, so familiar to him that he could recite their contents from memory.

'You had no such excuse at university,' she reminded him. 'I wrote then as well. But you did not answer those letters, either. It rather appeared to me that you had forgotten me.'

'Never,' he said fervently. That, at least, was the truth.

'Well, I will not allow it to happen again. Edinburgh is too far. You must stay close. And if you must teach, then teach me.'

He laughed, to cover the shock. It was not possible, for so many reasons. While he was not totally unwilling to share the information, he did not dare. She was a grown woman and not some curious girl. Discussing the intimate details of the human body would be difficult with any female. But with Evie, it would be impossible.

And if she was to marry, their circles would be so different that even casual conversation would be infrequent. Next to a duke, he would be little better than a tradesman.

'You know that is not proper,' he said at last.

'Your father would not allow it. Nor would your husband.' They both must remember that there would be another man standing between them.

And more than that.

He was forgetting himself again—and forgetting the reason he had to stay away. They could not be friends any more than they could be lovers. He had spent years away from her, known other women and prayed for a return to common sense. Nothing had dulled his feelings for her. The desire was just as strong and the almost palpable need to rush to her, catch her in his arms and hold her until the world steadied again. If she married, it would be no different. He would still want her. He would simply add the sin of adultery to an already formidable list.

He patted her hand in a way that showed a proper, brotherly affection. 'No, Evie. I cannot allow you to spin wild plans, as you did when we were children. I must go back to my life and you to yours.'

'But you are staying in London for a time, aren't you?' she said, looking up at him with the bluest of eyes, full of a melting hope.

'I had not planned to.' Why could he not manage a firmer tone? He'd made it seem like he might be open to persuasion.

'You must stay for the engagement ball. And the ceremony.'

As if that would not be the most exquisite torture. 'I do not know if that is possible.'

Her hand twisted, so that her fingers tightened on his. 'I will not allow you to go. Even if I must restrain you by force.' She should know that she had not the strength to do so. But she had tried it often enough, when they were young, tackling him and trying to wrestle him to the ground in a most unladylike fashion.

The idea that she might attempt it again sounded in his mind like an alarm bell.

'Very well,' he said with a sigh, if only to make her release his hand. 'But I expect I will leave soon after. Perhaps, instead of Scotland, I shall return to sea.'

'You mustn't,' she said, gripping him even more tightly before remembering herself and relaxing her hold. 'It takes you too far away from me for too long. And although you did not speak of it,

I am sure it must have been very dangerous. I would not have you put yourself at risk, again.'

It had been quite dangerous. He was sure that he could tell her stories for hours that would have her in awe. Instead, he said, 'Not really. It was a job. Nothing more than that. Unlike St Aldric, I must have employment if I am to live.' The words made him sound petulant. He should not be envious of a man that had been born to a rank he could never achieve.

She ignored the censure of the duke, which had been childish of him. 'You must have a practice on land. I will speak to father about it. Or St Aldric.'

'Certainly not! I am quite capable of finding my own position, thank you.' In any other life, an offer of patronage from a future duchess would have been just the thing he needed. But not this woman. Never her.

'You value your independence more than our friendship,' she said, and released his hand. 'Very well, then. If there is nothing I can say that will change your mind, I will bother you no further on the subject of your career.'

There was one thing, of course. Three words from her would have him on his knees, ready to do anything she might ask.

And since they were the three words neither of them must ever speak, he would go to Edinburgh or the ends of the earth, so that he might never hear them.

Chapter Three

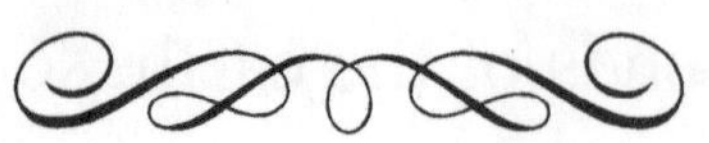

There was really nothing more to say. She had all but dismissed him, with her promise not to meddle in his affairs. Yet Sam was loathe to take leave of her. When would he get another such chance just to sit at her side, as they always used to? She was examining the box that held the spy-glass, as though it were the answer to some mystery.

And he was watching her hands caress it. Had they been so graceful when last he'd seen them? He could remember stubby fingers and ragged nails from too much time running wild with him. Today, she had not bothered with gloves and he could see the elegant taper of each digit that rested on the wood. He could sit there happily, staring at those hands for the rest of his life.

'This is where I find you? In the garden, flirting with another. I swear, Evelyn, you are harder to catch than a wild hare. I cannot leave you alone for a moment or you shall get away from me.'

The words came from behind them and Sam flinched as he guessed the identity of the intruder. The voice marked the end of any privacy they might have this afternoon. Or possibly for ever, assuming the duke had any brains. If Sam had been Evie's intended, he would never have allowed another man near her. He rose and turned to greet his newfound enemy face to face.

If Sam had been called to give a professional opinion on the man approaching them, he'd have proclaimed him one of the healthiest he had ever seen. Under his expensive clothing, St Aldric's form was symmetrical. There was not an ounce of fat and no sign that the perfection was achieved with padding or cinching. His limbs and spine were straight, his muscles well developed—skin, eyes, teeth and hair all clean, clear and shining with vigor. Likewise there were no wrinkles on his brow, of age or care, and no evidence in expression of anything but good humour. His gaze was benevolent intelligence, his step firm and confident. If Sam had been forced to express an opinion of another man's looks, he'd have called this one exceptionally handsome. From the toe of his boot to the top of his head, the fellow was the perfection of English manhood.

It made Sam even more conscious of how he must look in comparison. Lord Thorne might think him a threat to Evie's happiness. But with his worn blue coat, thin purse and modest future, a duke would hardly notice him. Unless Evelyn had grown to be as foolish as she was beautiful, she would have no trouble choosing the better man.

As if to prove his point, Evie rose as well and held out her hands to the duke. She smiled warmly and greeted him with genuine affection. 'St Aldric.'

'My dear.' He took her hands and held them for a moment, and Sam felt the uncomfortable pricking of jealousy and the punishment of being forgotten. She was pulling the other man forwards by the hand, just as she had lured Sam to the garden to sit beside her. It was yet another proof that the communion he had felt between them was nothing more than the warmth she showed all living things.

Now she was smiling back at him with proper, sisterly pride. 'I have waited long to introduce the two of you and now I have my opportunity. Your Grace, may I present Dr Samuel Hastings.'

'The one of whom you speak so fondly. And so often.' There was a fractional pause between the two sentences, as if to indicate jealousy, or perhaps envy of the attention she paid to him.

'Your Grace?' Sam bowed, giving a peer the required respect.

The duke was watching him in silence and Sam was sure, if they had shared something as egalitarian as a handshake, it would have become a test of strength. In it, St Aldric would have felt the roughness of the calluses on his hands made by a firm grip on a bone saw, then he would have been dismissed as not quite a gentleman.

'Doctor Hastings.' But it had not taken something so common as physical contact to do that. The less-than-noble honorific had been enough. The duke's frosty demeanour thawed into a handsome smile, now that he had assured himself of Sam's inferiority. Then St Aldric gave Evie another fond smile. 'I have been quite looking forwards to meeting this paragon you have been describing to me. I swear your face fairly lights up when you speak of him.'

'Because he is my oldest and dearest friend,' Evie said dutifully. 'We were raised together.'

As brother and sister. Why would she never say it? It would make life so much easier if she would understand the significance of that.

'We spent very little time apart until he went to university,' she added.

'To be a leech,' the duke replied blandly. It made Sam feel like a parasite.

'A physician,' Evie corrected, protective of his dignity. 'He was ever so clever when we took lessons together. Good at maths and languages, and fascinated by the workings of the body and all things natural. Sam is a born philosopher. I am sure he is most wonderful at his job.'

'And you have not seen him in all these years,' the duke reminded her. 'I shall try not to be too jealous of your obvious affection for him.' Then he stated the obvious, so that there might be no confusion. 'If Dr Hastings has not come back to sweep you up before now, the man has quite missed his chance.'

'I suppose he has,' Evie answered. She sounded unconcerned, but Sam suspected the words were a goad to action.

'Suppose?' St Aldric laughed again, willing to pretend that she had been joking. 'That is not nearly as confident as I wish you to be. Do you expect us to duel for you? I will call him out and we will see who is the better.' This too was more joke than threat.

'Do not talk nonsense,' Evie said hurriedly. 'I would think you both very foolish if you fought over me.'

'If it displeases you, then I shall not attempt it. He is a military man, after all. It would be even worse should Dr Hastings prove skilled enough to defeat me with a pistol.' The duke smiled at Sam, as though inviting him to join in the fun and prove that he had no feelings for her. 'With my luck, I would end with a ball in my shoulder that would have to be removed by the man who put it there. He would be doubly the hero and I would lose you twice as fast.'

'You have nothing to fear,' Evie repeated.

'Nor do you,' St Aldric reminded her softly and kissed her on the forehead.

There was no passion in it. It was delivered almost as a benediction. But Sam saw it for what it was. Even if there had been no public announcement, the woman between them was spoken for. In response, Sam gave St Aldric the slightest nod to prove that the message was understood.

Evelyn paid no more attention to the kiss than she would have to any other salute. But she was staring at the duke with the same teasing affection that she had shown to Sam only moments before. 'I see you have arrived empty handed again.'

Rather than chide her for her greediness, St Aldric laughed as though this was another old joke between them. 'I know you better than that, my dear. You would send me packing if I came without some sort of gift.'

Once again, Sam cursed himself for not being able to say those words to her himself. But it might ease his jealousy if St Aldric proved to be as shallow as Sam hoped, and gave her something that did not suit her.

It appeared that was not to be the case. The bulging pocket of his coat trembled slightly, though the duke did not move.

'What is it?' Evie said, eyeing the lump with curiosity. 'Give it to me this instant. It does not appear to be very happy where it is.'

'And that is why I brought it to you. I am sure it will be much happier, in your care.' He reached two fingers into the coat and withdrew a sniffling ginger kitten, placing it gently in Evie's lap.

'Oh, Michael.' Instantly captivated, she set Sam's spyglass aside and scooped the little thing up so that she could look at it, eye to eye. It blinked back at her, before letting out a nervous mew and settling down into the hollow of her hand. She stroked its head and nuzzled it to her cheek, smiling. 'It is too perfect.'

And Sam had to admit it was. Like the telescope, it held her attention in a way that a necklace never could. But unlike Sam's desperate good luck in finding something suitable already in his pocket, St Aldric had learned her preferences and planned in advance for this surprise.

She rewarded him with a smile so warm that Sam could swear he saw the duke colour with humble pleasure. It was sickening. Could not this interloper have behaved like the peer he was, pompous and demanding, blustering into this sacred space and defiling it so that Sam might hate him in good conscience? Could he have been a slightly less imposing physical specimen, with the beginnings of a paunch, or some spot or blemish?

Instead, he continued to be perfect. And he was looking down at Evie and the kitten as though he had never seen a lovelier sight.

'What shall I call you, little one?' She held it up again, staring into the grave green eyes. 'Something to suit your nature, for I am sure you shall be a great hunter, when you are old enough. Orion, perhaps.'

St Aldric cleared his throat. 'I should rather think Diana would be more appropriate.'

He was educated as well? A cursory knowledge of mythology and feline anatomy was not an indication of genius. But at least it proved that he was not some inbred dolt.

Evie turned the kitten in her hands and gave the underside a second look. 'I think you are right.' Then she turned it right way up and kissed it upon the head by way of a christening. 'Diana it is. And you shall have the run of the garden, a bowl of cream and, when you have lost your milk teeth, you shall have all the mice you can eat.'

'You will spoil it horribly,' Sam said, trying to be the gruff and grumbling older brother.

Evie gave him a disgusted look. 'It is not possible to spoil a thing by giving it too much affection. If I coddle her a bit, I am sure she will only become more devoted and do her job better. You could learn by that and not neglect your family for years at a time.' Then she smiled again at the kitten and the man who had given it to her.

It was like watching her hold out a gift of her own and then turn and give it to someone else. She was punishing him, deliberately favouring the duke. And though he was filled with the jealousy she wished for, he could do nothing to show it. He should not have come here. If her smiles were all for St Aldric, that was as it should be. There was no place for him any more.

And much as Sam might have wished to find fault with his rival, he could not. He was worthy of Evie. Evie was obviously fond of him. He had but to step out of the way and let nature take its course. These two would be married by summer's end.

All the more reason not to be trapped in the garden with the happy couple and sick to his stomach at the sight of love in bloom. He prayed for an excuse that might allow him to escape.

'Evelyn!' Lord Thorne called from the house, hurrying out to be with them. At any other time, Sam would have thought an interruption of his foster father as a sign that the situation had gone from bad to worse. But today it was a welcome relief.

'You have found her, then, your Grace?' Thorne gave a self-deprecating laugh and answered his own question. 'Of course you have. She was not lost, after all. And Sam?' His eyes widened with surprise that was actually annoyance. 'You are still with us? As I recall, you said you would be leaving.'

'I had other plans for him,' Evelyn said triumphantly. 'He tried to get away without so much as a hello. But I stopped him.'

'I am sure he could have escaped you, had he but tried.' Another warning from Thorne to mind his place. Sam could feel his normally placid temper stretch to a breaking point. He had a mind to tell the man aloud that he would leave immediately, if only to put an end to these continual reminders of his obvious inferiority.

'And he is staying at an inn, and not with us, as he should. It is truly horrible of him. I will not stand for it,' Evie added, in the same playful scolding tone she had been using on St Aldric.

'If the good doctor wishes to stay at an inn, it is not our place to correct him,' Thorne answered, putting the blame on Sam.

'Of course it is,' Evie said, unbothered. 'We are his family. I will allow nothing less than his sending for his baggage and moving back to his old room for the duration of his stay in London. I will have the space aired and made up for him immediately.' She rose and set the kitten on the bench, twining her arm with her father's. Though she might be his affectionate and loving daughter, she had a will of iron and was used to getting her way. If Sam did not go soon, she would work on Thorne without mercy until he gave her what she wanted. 'Come along, Papa, and add your voice to mine. I am sure Mrs Abbott will be quite cross with me for the sudden change in plans.' She was fairly dragging her father by the arm and back towards the house, lecturing him on hospitality while she was neglecting both her guests.

She tossed a smile in their direction, as though that would be more than enough to keep them, until she returned. 'If you gentlemen would spare our company? You must know each other better.'

'Of course,' St Aldric said, speaking for both of them. 'I am sure that Dr Hastings can entertain me in your absence.'

'I will leave Diana with you as well,' Evie said, as though she was not sure that Sam's company would suffice on its own. Then she fixed him with a cool stare. 'And do not move from this spot, Samuel Hastings, without taking leave of me. I still have not forgiven you for the last time you did.'

Nor had he forgiven himself. This time, he owed her a goodbye, if nothing else. He gave a grudging nod of agreement and she returned to take her father's arm. 'Do not fear. I will not be long.'

Chapter Four

'What is the meaning of this rudeness, Evelyn? You left St Aldric alone, when he came specifically to see you.' At her side, Evelyn could feel her father puffing in indignation like a tropical fish.

She smiled at him and added a loving hug and a doting look, ashamed of herself for this blatant manipulation. She had been taught by Aunt Jordan that a lady must use honey to catch flies. But sometimes she could not help but envy men their ability to catch flies with a reasonable argument. 'I did not leave St Aldric alone, Father. Sam was there.'

'That hardly signifies.' His grumbling was a last desperate attempt to rein her in. But since he had not been successful in twenty-one years, she had no real fear of punishment.

'I believe it does,' she said, quietly, still smiling, but renewing her grip on his arm and leading him down the hall to the library, shutting the door behind them so that there was no chance for a servant to hear what she wished to say. Then she checked the window that looked out on the garden to be sure that it was closed. No word of their conversation must reach the men talking there until she had confirmed her suspicions.

'A physician and a duke?' Father was shaking his head like a dog worrying a bone. 'The only reason that the two of them should speak is if the peer is ill, and you know for a fact that he is not. Unless… You have no fears, have you?' As usual, her father was thinking ahead to a future that she had not yet agreed to.

'Are you worried about my widowhood before I am even a bride?' she said with a raised eyebrow. 'It is nothing like that. St Aldric is perfectly healthy, as is obvious to all who see him. But Sam is a member of the family. I think it is important that the two get to know each other.

Don't you?' She looked expectantly at her father, hoping that he would not force her to badger the truth from him.

'If you assume that Hastings will play a part in your future, you harbour a misapprehension. We have discussed it and he is leaving London shortly. I doubt you will see him again.'

The finality of this statement was in direct opposition to her desires, so she ignored it. 'Hastings?' she chided. 'Really, Father. Now you are the one who is being rude. When did you cease to think of him as Sam? And for what reason? If there is some breach between the two of you, then I beg you to heal it, for my sake.'

'There is no breach,' her father insisted, probably afraid that she would resort to tears. 'But we have an understanding, he and I. And what has been done is all for your sake, I assure you.'

As if she needed protection from Sam. The idea was quite ridiculous and not worth mentioning. 'I am more concerned with Sam and his future, Father. So should you be.'

'He is seeing to that well enough, without my help,' her father said. Perhaps he was simply hurt that the boy he had raised could manage to prosper without him.

'His success is a credit to your early tutelage, I am sure.' She must turn the topic, for she wished to close the breach and not widen it. Her father appeared somewhat mollified at the thought that he had contributed to Sam's obvious success. 'And I see no reason that he cannot stay here with us, while he is in London.'

'He does not wish to,' her father said, firmly.

'I am happy to see that you have no objection,' she said with another smile. One thing did not imply the other. But it was better to let him think her illogical than to allow argument. Then she added, as though in afterthought, 'Once he is here, it will give you a chance to tell him what you know of his true parentage.'

'I?' That had caught him unawares, she was sure. He was flustered out of countenance and almost beyond speech. It took several seconds for him to manage a proper denial. 'I know nothing. And whatever Samuel Hastings has told you on the subject is clearly a lie.'

'He…told me?' She gave a bat of her lashes to

reinforce the innocence of her discovery. 'He did not tell me anything. But I needed no great wit to draw my conclusion. I have my own eyes, if I wish to see the truth. You had best give him the whole story, if you have not already.'

'I have no idea what you mean,' said her father, in the slow and deliberate way that people sometimes used to deny the obvious.

Eve sighed and gave up on honey, preferring to catch this particular fly with a swatter. 'Then I will explain it to you. I have had suspicions for quite some time. But it was only until just now, in the garden, that I was sure. When they are seen together by others, someone will remark on the resemblance between them. From there it is only a short step to seeing that the Duke of St Aldric and Dr Samuel Hastings are as alike as brothers.'

'Evie, you mustn't meddle in this.' It was the same weak prohibition that he tried whenever she stepped out of bounds.

Since she knew there were no consequences to disagreeing, it would meet with the same lack of success. She continued. 'You were a good friend of the old duke when he was alive, were you not?'

'Of course, but...'

'And mightn't he have asked you a favour, at one point in your life, when you and mother feared that you would be childless?' In case she had been too direct, she larded the question with more feminine sweetness. 'I only ask because I know there will be gossip.'

'There will be none if Hastings leaves, as he is promised to,' her father said stubbornly. He had not affirmed or denied her theory. But evasiveness was an answer.

'It is hardly fair to Sam, if you make him leave London just because of the duke.' Nor was it fair to her. She would not lose him again, over something that should not matter to anyone. 'If the estrangement between you is nothing more than a fear of making this revelation, you had best get it over with. Since I love both men, I mean to keep them close to me for as long as I am able.' She smiled again and offered a bait that she doubted her father could resist. 'I am sure that St Aldric would welcome the news. He has spoken frequently of the burden of being the only remaining member of his family. You would gain much favour by telling him what he longs to hear.'

'Revelation of a natural son…' her father stopped himself before revealing the truth '…if there were such, would do nothing to change his status as the last of the line.'

'It would change the contents of his heart,' Eve argued. 'I know his spirit; it is generous to a fault. He would want to share his wealth with his father's son. And it would at least make him cease his jokes about duels between them. Imagine his reaction, should they fight for some reason, and not learn the truth until after one of them had been injured.'

'For some reason?' She had pushed too far. Her father had spotted the hole in her argument and made his escape. 'Really, Evelyn. Do not play the naïf. You know perfectly well that they would be fighting over your attentions. If an accident occurs, it will be your fault and not mine. You must send Hastings away. I have assured myself that the man is too sensible to harbour false hope on a match between you. And neither should you.'

'I am not offering false hope.' There was nothing false about it. After the time spent in the garden, the hope she felt was quite real. As was her conviction about the identity of Sam's father. 'I am simply attempting to right a wrong, before it goes further. It pains both men and does no credit to you.'

'You are meddling in things you cannot understand,' he said, patting her on the hand and treating her like the child he still believed she was. 'If this is the reason you were impolite to St Aldric, then I am sorry to disappoint you. I have nothing to say on the matter, because there is nothing to say.'

Had she failed to persuade him? This happened so rarely that, for a moment, she suspected she might have been wrong. Perhaps there was no secret to reveal. 'Father…'

'Go!' He pointed a finger back towards the garden, once again secure in his control of the situation. 'Send Dr Hastings on his way before the duke tires of his company. Visit with St Aldric, as he desires. I have no intention of helping you out of the muddle you are making. This discussion is at an end and will not be repeated. Now, go.' Her father's lips were set in a firm line, as if to show her that no more words would pass between them until she had fulfilled her obligation to him, to society and to the duke.

But he was giving no thought to Sam's needs. If he would not, then someone must, or he would be back on a boat and out of her life for ever. 'Very well, then. I will talk to St Aldric. But you are wrong about the rest, Father. We will speak of this again and, next time, you will tell the truth.' She would worry him with it night and day, if necessary. But she would have her way, and Sam would know his brother.

In Evelyn's absence, an awkward silence had fallen between the two men. It was hardly surprising. Sam seldom had cause to speak to a man of such great rank and no right to initiate conversation. The duke had no reason to speak to him. It left the pair of them staring morosely at the kitten on the bench until the thing stumbled to the edge and off, wandering into the grass to stalk and pounce on crickets.

Now there was not even an excuse for the silence. It seemed that St Aldric was not content with this, for he was searching about him as though expecting to see an opening to a conversation. At last he offered, 'Evelyn says you were educated in Scotland, and after you took to the sea.'

'Indeed, your Grace.' Sam shifted uneasily, clasping his hands behind his back.

'The navy is an unusual choice for such a well-educated man. But I cannot fault your adventurous spirit.'

Sam was tempted to announce that he had not requested an opinion, but he had only one reason to dislike this man and no reason at all to be rude to him. Excessive fondness for Evie was no excuse for a lack of respect to the peerage. 'The navy is an economical way to see the world,' Sam admitted. 'The prize money from ships taken was sufficient to make up for the lack of a medical practice.' It would be nothing to the holdings of a duke, but it had been more than satisfactory for Sam.

The duke nodded approval. 'The captain of the *Matilda* was ambitious.'

It was the truth, but St Aldric had stated it as though he already knew. Had he made an effort to discover this, or had Evie revealed it to him? 'A very ambitious captain indeed, your Grace.' He'd made enough to retire and return to land, and to have a house and family, should he wish for one.

'Your record is admirable,' the duke continued. 'Other than a brief flirtation with the church of Rome, while you were in Spain.'

So he had read the record, then. And the warning put there by the captain, for the time he had spent conversing with priests. 'It was curiosity. Nothing more.' And a desire to find a cure for his spiritual affliction, or at least absolution, from a clergy that was bound to secrecy. In the end, the priest had looked at him with pity and disgust, and given him beads and prayer, almost as Sam might have prescribed a pill.

It had done no good.

'It is strange that you have taken such an interest in *my* interest.' Sam allowed himself the candid observation. The meddling in his affairs by this stranger annoyed him. 'I do not mean to bother Evelyn with it, if that is what you fear.'

'Not at all, sir,' the duke said hastily. 'I merely wished to take your measure.'

'Then consider it done. I am what you see before you. No more, no less. In the future, if you have a question, you might ask me directly and I will answer it honestly and to the best of my ability. For Evelyn's sake, if for no other reason.' Did invoking her name make the words sound any less rude?

'I see,' the duke said.

'I wonder if you do?' Sam said, too tired of the games they were playing to dissemble. 'I might as well have sworn to you on all that is holy. Such an oath would have had no more strength than my wish for Eve's continued well-being. No matter what you might suspect, I want what is best for her.' And then he admitted grudgingly, 'If what I am hearing is true, she is on the verge of a fortunate match.'

Rather than answer this, the duke merely shrugged. It was a strange, rather boyish response from one so confident. 'I have hopes. But it is up to the lady, is it not?'

'I wish her well,' Sam added. 'She deserves the best that life offers. I have no reason to think she is not about to receive it.'

The duke gave him a long, slow look in response to this, as though trying to decide if he believed it. At last, he answered, 'I am happy to hear you say so. Should I be the future you predict, I shall do my best to be worthy of her.'

This made Sam respond with an equally probing look. He could have understood a warning to stay away. But this behaviour seemed to indicate that the duke sought this approval. It was not necessary.

The silence fell between them again. It was even heavier this time, like the exhausted rest of men who had fought each other and were waiting between rounds to regain their breath.

Into the tense pause came Eve. As though she had not been between them the whole time, thought Sam with an ironic smile.

She was smiling as well, totally unaware of the direction their conversation must have gone. 'I have returned to you,' she announced. 'I hope that my absence has given the pair of you a chance to become acquainted.'

'You were gone barely ten minutes, Evelyn,' the duke responded. 'It was hardly enough time to establish a lasting friendship.'

'But you spoke,' she said as though prodding a wayward child through his lessons. 'And you found him to be all that I have said?'

It made Sam wonder just what Eve had said of him.

'I did not doubt your description,' St Aldric answered. 'But, yes.'

'Then did you tell him what we discussed?'

'I was a topic of discussion?' Sam interrupted. He did not like being talked about. It was almost as annoying as being the subject of an enquiry.

'I simply made clear to St Aldric how your career worried me,' Evie replied, sitting between them in the space the kitten had occupied. She reached out and clasped his hand. 'You were gone so long, Sam. I missed you. And do not tell me the navy is not dangerous. Even with Napoleon defeated, it must be. There are storms and pirates, and all manner of accidents that might befall you. Suppose you took ill? Who would treat the physician?'

'Evie.' Now she was coddling him and doing it in front of the duke. He added embarrassment to the host of other discomforts she caused.

'I wondered if something might be done to persuade you to stay ashore.'

'Do you not think that I am best able to decide for myself?' Sam said, as gently as possible.

'I told her as much,' St Aldric said with a sigh. 'But she did not wish to hear it.' For a moment, they were brothers in arms against a foe as tenacious as Bonaparte. But having fought both, Sam credited Evie as more stubborn than the whole French army.

'I am tired of people ignoring my letters and dismissing my fears,' Eve said, eyes narrowed and jaw set. 'Samuel Hastings, you are risking your life at sea and there is no reason for it. I have been quite beside myself, praying for your return. A practice on land will be safer. Something must be arranged for you.'

Sam took a breath before speaking, trying to

keep his temper for her sake. 'As I told you before, I prefer to make my own way. My early life was spent beholden to your father and it was difficult.' More difficult than she could possibly imagine. 'The debts of gratitude I incurred are something that can never be repaid.'

'You need not be grateful for a job,' she snapped back. 'I am sure you are skilled enough to merit this position. It is an opportunity, nothing more. You will prove your worth by your service. I have spoken to St Aldric and he is agreed.' She gave the duke a warning look that said this had best be the truth, if he knew what was good for him. And then her expression changed to sort of smile that no man could resist and she took the duke's hand, giving it the same warm squeeze that she had given Sam. 'It is all settled. You will come to Aldricshire with us and act as Michael's personal physician.'

For a moment, the anger was stunned out of him. Any doctor in England would be overjoyed with such a post. St Aldric was young and strong, and of an amiable nature that bespoke a long and pleasant career in his service. It would mean a life of comfort and a chance to keep a wife and children in luxury.

As long as he was willing to keep Evelyn's husband fit and healthy. Perhaps he would be required to watch over her, as she grew big with another man's child, and stand by in approval as their brood increased. And now she was holding both their hands and looking from one to the other as though it would be possible to make the three of them into one happy family.

'No.' He made no effort to hide his disgust as he pulled his hand out of her grasp and stood, turning and backing away from the pair on the bench. 'You ask too much of me, Evie.' He looked to the man beside her, trying to maintain a frigid courtesy. This idea was no fault of the duke's, but it explained his rude questioning of moments before. He probably feared that Sam was the sort of man who would use Evie's fondness to his own betterment. 'I apologise, your Grace, but I must respectfully refuse the offer.' Perhaps St Aldric could explain it to her. The man must have guessed his feelings, if Thorne had not already explained the situation.

He looked at Evie, whose beautiful eyes were beginning to fill with tears, and then he backed away from her, towards the house. 'And I should take my leave as well. It is long past the time I meant to go. You persuaded me to tarry. But I should not have listened.'

Lead us not into temptation... The words of the prayer echoed in his mind.

But they offered no protection from the stricken look on her face. 'Sam, wait...'

If she spoke another word, he would weaken. He would wipe those tears and agree to anything that might make her smile again. She would have him moved into the house by evening, sleeping scant feet from her bedroom door.

'I cannot.' *Must not.* 'Not another moment. Good day to you, Lady Evelyn. And you as well, your Grace. And goodbye.'

Chapter Five

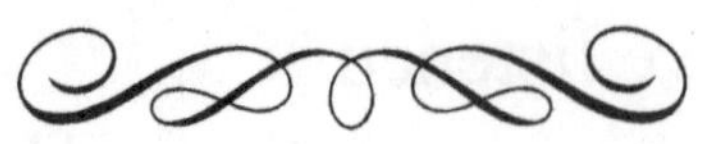

Evie watched the London streets passing by outside the carriage window and tapped her foot impatiently on the boards beneath the seat. It was really too much to bear.

Before making her come out, it had been drummed into her by Aunt Jordan that her future depended on her ability to be pleasant. It was almost as important as looks and much more important than intelligence. Men might marry a beautiful ninnyhammer, as long as she hung on their words and did not correct them. But a shrew would be a shrew, long after looks faded.

So Eve had done her best to be good company. And though she could not keep herself from arguing, she always did it with a smile on her face. Perhaps that was why the men in her life were treating her like a child, alternately scolding and humouring her, thinking that they could render her agreeable to what they wanted. Because she did not look angry, they did not believe she was serious.

Father was clearly lying about what he knew of Sam. Sam was equally evasive when it came to the truth of his feelings for her, changing from hot to cold and back again so suddenly that she could hardly understand him.

And St Aldric? She smiled in spite of herself. He would appoint the devil himself as a personal physician if he thought it would bring her any closer to accepting his offer. At least the man was consistent. But since she did not love him, his opinion hardly signified.

The carriage pulled to a stop outside the inn where Sam was staying. It was another piece of nonsense that he had refused his old room, remaining aloof in a place that could not be half as nice as home. Even worse, she had been forced to worm the location of it from the coachman who had taken him away. Sam had left no direction for her and her father had announced that he had no idea where to find the man, nor was he bothered by his ignorance.

Now that she was here, she told her Banbury tale to the hostler and was shown to the room where Sam had gone to ground. She knocked smartly on the door and heard the answering 'come' from the other side. Perhaps he was expecting a maid with his dinner.

She smiled to herself. He was certainly not expecting her. But he must learn to like surprises. She opened the door and swept into the room, her smart day dress swirling around her. 'Good afternoon, Dr Hastings. I have come to continue our discussion in private.'

'Evie.' He rose from the desk where he had been seated and a prayer book tumbled to the floor, brushed from the table in front of him.

She had not known him to be particularly religious, but people altered with time. He probably did not think of her as a sophisticated débutante. When he'd left, she had been a scapegrace companion with manners no better than his. But the change in her should not have shocked him this much. He was backing away from the door as though he meant to brace his shoulders against the wall. He had the look of a startled animal.

But a thoroughly masculine animal, if she was to be honest. He was out of his coat, with his shirt sleeves rolled up to keep the grime from his cuffs. She could see muscles in those arms, and shoulders more broad and strong than she'd imagined. She swallowed and remembered, for just a moment, why one did not court impropriety by forcing one's way into a gentleman's room for a private interview.

But the gentleman was Sam. And no matter what might happened between them, she did not fear it.

'What are you doing here?' he asked, wary. 'And why were you even allowed above stairs? The innkeeper will think you a common trollop for behaving so.'

'Nonsense,' she said and gave him a wink, trying to coax a smile from him. 'I told him that we were family. Is it not natural for a sister to visit a brother?'

He made a strange, strangled noise, as though

he could not quite master his speech, and then said weakly, 'It was still very wrong of you.'

'But I could not allow you to leave me in anger. I do not want to part this way. I do not want to part at all.' She glanced at the sea chest on the floor. It was clear that he was packing again. 'And I certainly do not want you to go as you did before, without a word.'

For a moment, her voice sounded strange as well. If she was not careful, she would break down in front of him and beg him to stay. Excess emotion was effective against Father. But Sam would likely think she was shamming and put her out of the room.

She conquered the tears, before they could escape. Running down the back of her throat, they tasted very like the ones she had shed when he'd first left her. She did not cry any more. Gentleman might be moved by a weeping woman, but they did not like her nearly as well as a smiling one. She dropped her head a bit so that she might appear demure and properly sorry for getting above herself. 'I will talk no more of finding you a position. I will not meddle at all. But you promised you would stay for the wedding. Remember? You promised. You cannot break your word to me, just because of a silly misunderstanding. Forgive me.' She looked up through her lashes and held out a hand to him. Contrition, helplessness, and a hint of flirtation should bring him round.

He ignored the hand, back still firmly against the wall. 'There is nothing to forgive. What you did was out of concern for me and I thank you for attempting to help, even if I must refuse. I will do as you ask and stay for the wedding. I will even buy a new coat and have my neckcloth properly tied for it, so that I do not shame you before St Aldric.'

His expression was frozen and his tone wooden. He looked and sounded as false as she felt, trying to snare him with her feminine wiles. He paused, wetting his lips before speaking again, as though it had been necessary to prepare himself for the answer. 'Now when is this wedding you are so eager for me to attend?'

She smiled in triumph. 'I really have no idea. I have not said yes, you remember. But if you mean to leave as soon as I am wed, I suspect it shall take me some time to decide.'

He lurched forwards as though about to give her a good shaking for her impudence, then regained control and ran his fingers through his hair. 'Evelyn, I swear, your behaviour is enough to drive a sane man to madness.'

'So I have been told,' she said with another smile. 'It is good to see that you are not unaffected by it.' She took a step closer to him, pressing her advantage. 'We were quite close at one time, though you work very hard to deny it.'

'Like siblings,' he said firmly.

She shook her head. He must have known how she'd felt about him. She had made no effort to hide her love. But he had given her no chance to elicit some promise from him, before he went off to school, so that she would know to wait for his return. Now that they were alone, there would be no better time. 'You were always more than a brother to me, Sam.'

'But you were always my dear little sister,' he said, stubbornly. 'And I am very proud to think that I will soon have to call you "Your Grace".

Or I will once you stop stringing poor St Aldric along.'

'I cannot accept him while there is still a question as to where my heart might lie,' she said.

He flinched. 'Surely such questions were answered long ago, Evelyn.'

'When you left me with no explanation?' she supplied.

'You knew I was to go away to school.'

'But I did not expect you to run the whole way. Nor did I expect you to run again today, in the middle of a simple conversation about your future.'

'A future you wished to choose for me,' he reminded her.

'And you are seeking a different one?' Perhaps it was with some other girl that felt the same way as she did. If it was another woman, why could he not just tell her? If it was to spare her pain, he had misjudged the situation. A simple answer for this rejection was bound to be better than not knowing.

And if there was another, the key to his absence was right here in the room with him. The other woman, if she was smart, would not have wanted him to forget that someone waited for his return. There must be a lock of hair, a miniature or some other token of her affection. Eve had but to find it and understand. And there before her was the sea chest and doctor's bag, waiting to be explored.

She trailed her fingers along the edge of the open chest and then turned to it suddenly, dropping to her knees to examine the contents.

There was no sign of another woman here. The box in front of her contained nothing but the tools of his profession.

It was novel enough that he had a trade, for most gentlemen did not. Eve tended the folks around their country home quite efficiently without a doctor's help, but she did it with little more than instinct, herbs and a needle and thread from her sewing box. It was charity and not real work at all.

But here before her were all the things that a trained physician might have at his disposal. To Eve, it was a revelation. She had read about the uses of such instruments in the books on medicine that she had got, but she had never seen them.

These were arrayed neatly, carefully, immaculate in their cleanliness and as ordered as idols in a temple. Lancets with smooth tortoiseshell handles, the gleaming steel of bone saws and drills, the terrifying razor edge of scalpels and the curved needles threaded with silk and gut. Beneath them, in neat rows, were cobalt-blue medicine bottles and the weird globes of the leech jars.

The third layer was a collection of more esoteric items, harder to pack, but obviously well used. A syringe made of hollow bone, ivory-and-silver medicine spoons and forceps. She examined each one in turn.

'Are you searching for something, Evelyn?' Sam had been so silent that she had almost forgotten him as she explored. But it seemed that her curiosity had relaxed him. He was no longer pinned to the wall, but standing just behind her. His voice had changed as well. The strangled desperation had changed to a familiar combination of disapproval, amusement, resignation and affection.

She wanted to turn and answer honestly. *Yes, I am searching for the key to understanding you.* Instead, she was almost as truthful. 'I am curious about your profession.' She turned to face him and sat on the floor, her legs tucked under.

'And once again, you prove that the years have not changed you. You always were a horrible little snoop.' He relaxed enough to sit down on the end of the bed. 'Is there anything you wish me to explain?'

'I know most of them,' she admitted.

'You do?' This seemed to surprise him.

'I have studied,' she admitted. 'I ordered the same texts you used in Edinburgh and read them cover to cover.'

Another man might have questioned her ability to understand them. But all that Sam said was, 'Does your father know?'

It was difficult to meet his gaze and admit the truth. Eve had not thought of herself as a deceptive person, when he had left her. Although she often disagreed with her father, she never set out to disobey him. But she had suspected in this it would be necessary and had kept the extent of her knowledge a secret from him. 'You know he does not. He would never have approved of it. He thinks I tend to the sick in the same way other women do, by bringing broth and good wishes, and the sort of herbal tinctures that Mother would have used had she survived. But I prefer to be more scientific about it.' Then a thought occurred to her. 'You will not tell him, will you?'

Sam laughed. 'Of course not.' And then he grew serious. 'Nor will I tell St Aldric. I doubt he is expecting a wife with such *outré* hobbies.'

If Sam loved her as she hoped, he could use the information to his advantage and spoil her chances with the duke. Instead, he was being noble. She sighed. 'The ways of men are very confusing. They have no care if we women meddle with illnesses, as long as we do it in ignorance. Do they not want people to recover?' She tipped her head to the side and watched Sam for an honest reaction as she asked the next question. 'What do you think of my dabbling? Am I wrong to want to practise what I can read clear on the page?'

He thought for a moment. 'I do not think I approve. There are many things I have seen in the service of medicine that I would not wish upon you. But I also know how difficult it is to dissuade you when you take an idea into your head. You have your own mind, Evie. No amount of disapproval on my part is likely to change it.' But the fact of the matter did not seem to frustrate or anger him. He was looking at her with the calm acceptance that she had hoped to see.

'Do you think I might make a decent physician?'

'The colleges will not train you, of course,' he said. 'But if they would, you are quick witted enough. You say you know the contents of my bag?'

She nodded. 'Of course.' She held up a tool. 'Forceps, to deliver babies. They are unnecessary, you know. The majority of births can be sorted out in other ways, if one is patient and has small hands.'

His eyes widened. 'You speak from experience?'

'Do you not remember our old country home? Thorne Hall is quite remote. The nearest doctor is miles away and we have learned to manage without a physician. I have grown to be quite a capable midwife, Dr Hastings.'

'And you limit yourself to that?' She had feared censure from him. But the question was asked with good-natured resignation, as though he already knew the answer.

'Perhaps I am more deeply involved in care than some people would wish,' she admitted. 'And perhaps I go more frequently to sick beds and birthing rooms than propriety requires. It is not as if I take money for the things I do.'

'Well, then…' he said, with an ironic smile. 'As long as you are no threat to my business.'

'No threat at all. And I suspect you have little practice with childbirth, if you have been on a ship full of men.' She set the forceps aside. 'Especially if you rely on these things. There is a place for them, of course. But most times I can do without them.'

He bowed his head to hide his smile. 'Then I yield to your superior experience in that part of the field. What else do you think to teach me?'

She pointed to the drill. 'This is for the trepanning of the skull. And here are the implements that scrape away the scalp and lift the bones from the wound.' She picked it up and gave the handle a turn. The thought of saving a person by drilling holes into their head was really quite amazing. 'Did you ever have to do such a thing?'

He laughed again. 'You have not changed at all, Evie. Your curiosity is as gruesome as ever. Yes, I have used it. Once successfully. Once not.' As though he wished to change the subject he advanced to the chest and pulled out an ebony tube. 'But I am sure you will not recognise this.'

She turned it over in her hands, looking for some clue to indicate its purpose. 'I have no idea.'

'That is not surprising. I suspect I have one of the few in England. I got it off a French surgeon on a prize ship we took. It takes the place of the percussion hammer, when sounding the lungs and listening to the heart.'

'How wondrous. You must show me.' She leaned forwards on her knees and held it out to him.

Something about this alarmed him. He stared at it for a moment and then at her. Then he took a breath, swallowed and placed one end against the bare skin above her bodice, then gingerly put his ear to the other. He moved the tube to several locations on her chest, requested that she breathe deeply each time and, with a scholarly nod, pronounced her sound. He withdrew with obvious relief.

So the nearness of her frightened him, did it? He had put on his best professional demeanour before attempting to examine her. But she had been well schooled in breaking down a man's objections. Those lessons would do for a drawing room, but with Sam she could be more direct. She smiled, sweetly. 'Now I must do you.' She took the tube away from him without waiting for permission. Then she undid several of the buttons on his waistcoat and spread the opening of his shirt hiding under the cravat.

'Evelyn!' He tried to back away from her and bumped into the headboard of the bed behind him.

She laughed. 'Oh, Sam. Do not be such a girl.' And then she leaned forwards to listen.

The sounds were strange and hollow, compared

to simply putting one's head to the chest of the patient, but the clarity was uncanny. As she listened, she heard the slight hitch in respiration, as though he could not manage to breathe normally. His heartbeat, compared to what she considered normal, was hard and rapid. For a moment, it worried her. Perhaps he was ill. Had his absence concealed some physical problem?

Or the rapid beat might be the sign she had hoped for. She put her hand on the bare skin of his chest to steady the tube and felt his breathing stop all together, even though his heart was racing.

It was her. He might pretend otherwise, but to have her near affected him in ways he could not control.

To test the theory, she moved her hand again and felt his heart jump. Then she looked up at him with a long slow smile.

He looked back with an expression she might have described as shattered.

'Why, Dr Hastings…' she removed the tube, but left her hand flat against the warm bare skin of his chest '…you are most excitable today.'

'Evie.' It was the warning tone of someone afraid of getting caught in an indiscretion.

She ignored it. 'Samuel?' She scratched her nails lightly against the skin of his chest, amazed at her own boldness, and waited for his reserve to crack.

Instead, he gripped her hand and removed it from his person, arranging his clothes to hide the place she had touched. 'Do not behave nonsensically. If someone were to discover you touching a man that way, it would do no good to claim it began as an interest in medicine. You would be quite ruined.'

'I am not touching any man,' she explained patiently, kneeling at his feet. 'It is just you.'

'Just me.' He let out a resigned sigh. 'You must remember we are grown now, Evelyn. The games that might have seemed quite natural twenty years ago are no longer proper.'

'Are there other games that might be more appropriate?' It was a daring question and she wondered how he might answer it.

'No.' He wet his lips and swallowed, as though it was an effort to talk to her.

'Just what is it that makes you so afraid of me, Sam?'

'Afraid?' He was parroting back her words, stalling for time, but it was clear from his expression that she had been right. He was terrified.

She leaned closer and put her hands on his knees, to look up into his face. If it was rejection he feared, he would not receive it. 'Have I changed so much, Sam? Because I never used to frighten you. You even kissed me once,' she reminded him.

'Did I?' He looked away from her, at the sea chest on the floor. 'I hardly remember it.'

'I remember it all too well. It was a week before you went away. We were in the garden. It was a morning, in summer. We were playing at games. I hid. When you caught me, you held me by the waist. Your eyes went very serious for a moment, then you pulled me close and kissed me on the mouth.'

'Ah, yes.' If possible he looked even more uncomfortable.

'And shortly after that, you left me to go to school.'

'It was but a bit of foolishness on my part. We were both very young, were we not?'

'I was fifteen,' she reminded him. 'Some girls are already married by then.'

'And now you are twenty-one. And likely to make a much better marriage than you might have, had you rushed into it at such a young age.' He said it as though he was trying to convince himself.

'I might be married to a physician now, had he asked me.'

'Evie.' Was that all he could manage to say to her? This time her name sounded just as sad, but full of longing as well.

'Since you will not speak plainly, I must,' she said, 'so that you cannot pretend to misunderstand me. If you offer, I will accept. If you wish it, I will go with you to Gretna tonight.'

'St Aldric…' he said, almost choking on the name.

'Is nothing to me,' she said, laying a hand against his cheek. 'Not compared to you.'

Finally his strength failed. He laid his own hand over hers, pressing her palm to his mouth.

His lips were hot against her skin. Even hotter as they met hers when he released her hand and pulled her forwards to take her lips.

And if she had thought this kiss would be like the one that they had already shared, she was proved wrong. He opened her mouth with a steady pressure and his tongue touched hers, advancing and retreating. At first it was a gentle tide, but it grew to a storm and she gave herself to it, trembling. She clung to his body and he held her there, between his legs so that she could feel his manhood growing against her belly. The thought of it pressing into her made her moan into his mouth.

He was aroused. She had but to give in to him and soon he would be beyond control. There would be no hesitation on her part. When the moment came, she would succumb. Once they had lain together, he would never leave her again.

She pressed his hand against her breast, urging him to stroke it through her gown. At the merest touch, he grew harder. He raised his other hand, kneading both, as if to prove that every inch of her body belonged to him. His kisses took on a desperate quality, as though he was trying to reach into her soul with each thrust of his tongue so that he might claim that as well.

She had imagined giving herself in passive submission, but suddenly she needed more than that. She wanted his hands on her bare skin and his body filling the wet empty place between her legs. As she knelt before him, he trapped her body between his thighs. So she ran her hands over them, back and forth, each time growing closer to their apex.

Her palms itched to caress him. It would not take much more than a touch, she was sure, and he would be irrevocably hers. Her fingertips grazed him, once, twice, three times through the cloth, and then they settled on the buttons of his breeches.

He pushed her away suddenly, scrambling back on the bed as though he could not put enough distance between them. His expression was wild, eyes fixcd and staring, lips drawn back, as his head shook once in an emphatic 'no'. Then he wiped his mouth with the back of his hand. It was as gesture of revulsion.

He pointed towards the door.

'I don't understand,' she whispered. She was near tears again. She swallowed hard to stop them. Crying was the lowest type of female trick. She would not give in to it with Sam, no matter how much she hurt. 'If you love me…'

'It is not love,' he said with finality, cold and professional again. 'I doubt I am even capable of the feeling. But if you value me, as you say you do, get up off your knees and get out of this room.'

'Leave you?' Now that she had finally found him, he wanted her to go?

'Marry St Aldric. Be safe and happy. But for God's sake, woman, go away and leave me in peace.' He stood and grabbed her again, but it was not for another kiss. Instead, he hauled her up off the floor and spun her away from him. Then he opened the door and pushed her through it and out in the hall.

The oak panel slammed behind her, cutting off her words of apology.

* * *

You must understand, my boy, it is quite impossible...

Sam looked wildly around the room, searching for the bottle that he had already packed. Rum. Stinging, harsh and nothing like her kiss. He pulled the cork and took a mouthful, swished it and spit it into the basin, expelling the memory of her taste.

Nothing he had seen in his studies at land or at sea could explain the feelings coursing through him now. He understood the pumping of the blood, the mechanical and chemical processes and increases in humour that led to arousal and release.

But none of it explained the demon that possessed him, the maggot in his brain that made him want the one woman he could not have.

It is my fault really. I should not have raised you together, as I did. At the very least, I should have made clear the relationship between you, to prevent this misunderstanding...

Lord Thorne's words were as fresh in his mind now as they had been on the day he had heard them. And they offered no more comfort now than they had then.

Your birth was the mistake of a youthful man. My wife was understanding, of course. She agreed that we should take you in. A natural son might ease her loneliness. We had no child of our own. And when, finally, we were blessed, she did not survive long enough to know our Evelyn.

Why could they not have left him where he was? If duty needed to be done, it could have been done at a distance, with a series of discreet and anonymous payments to guardians and schools.

And then he might never have met Evelyn Thorne. A life with no Evie in it was his greatest desire, and his worst nightmare, hopelessly mixed.

I could have acknowledged you. Perhaps I should have...

Before puberty, perhaps. Sam laughed bitterly at the thought, and took another swig of the rum to wash the bitterness away. If he had understood what Evie was to him, then he would never have fallen in love with her.

And as he had done so many nights before, he went to the desk and took up his beads and a Bible so worn from use that it fell open automatically to Leviticus.

The nakedness of thy sister, the daughter of thy father, or the daughter of thy mother, whether born at home, or born abroad even their nakedness thou shalt not uncover.

He prayed, as he always did, for strength and for forgiveness.

Chapter Six

'Evelyn! Stop tormenting that poor kitten and see to your hem. I swear, girl, you cannot keep the stitches straight if you allow a beast to swipe at the edge of the linen.'

'I am sorry, Aunt Jordan.' Evie glanced at the work in her lap and tried to raise any interest in it. These sessions of needlework were another concession to her father's wish that she behave like a young lady. On the few evenings when she had no other engagement, she was forced to endure them, along with critiques of her deportment. As usual, they were a trial both to her and the poor aunt charged with teaching her.

She set the shirt aside and lifted the kitten into her lap, offering it the end of the string to chase. 'It is hardly fair to blame Diana for my indifferent needlework. I was equally bad at it before she arrived.'

'Your manners have improved much in the last years,' her aunt reminded her. 'And you are on the cusp of success with St Aldric. Snaring a peer is much more challenging than plain sewing. Your stitching would improve as well, if you would but make an effort at it.'

If it was put to some other purpose than making shirts, then perhaps she would try harder. She remembered the pages in Sam's text books that explained suturing and wondered if large wounds were more difficult than the cuts she had closed. The stitches would need to be bigger, of course, and more numerous. As she poked at the linen, she imagined the resistance of skin, and the difficulties created when the subject flinched…

'Evelyn!'

The needle slipped and she pricked her finger instead of the cloth. She waved her hand in the air for a moment, trying to shake the pain away, then held it high to keep the drop of blood that formed from falling on the work. This sent her mind to the various methods to staunch bleeding, and the efficacy of causing it when one had an excess of certain humours.

Not that she would need any of this information as the wife to a duke. But that had never been her plan, not even from the first. She had studied and prepared so that, on the day that Sam finally realised his mistake and came home to her, she might prove herself a useful helpmeet to him. If she understood his work, then they would always have something to talk about.

But he had barely given her time to display any of her hardwon knowledge to him. While in his rooms, she had allowed the physical side of the conversation to come to the fore, proving to him in a most unladylike way that she understood biology.

Perhaps she would have fared better if she had put the stethoscope back into the chest and turned the conversation to the use of leeches and cupping as the old Evie would have. Or behaved as the charming and witty young lady Aunt Jordan had taught her to be. Instead, she had tried to combine the two and it had been a disaster.

She had offered herself to the man she loved—

and he had rejected her. Though she might deny it to herself, it was what she had feared might happen. Sometimes, six years of silence meant exactly what they appeared to. Girlish sureties might owe more to fairy tales and fantasy than they did to truth. There had always been a chance that the kiss she remembered as loving and passionate was nothing more than a peck on the cheek. She had been prepared for that.

But not for what had occurred. If anything, she had remembered the past too innocently. Or had his passion grown to conflagration during their separation?

And yet he denied it. He did not seem to know love from lust. She was sure, after all they had been through together, that she did. Why else had she waited so many years for him to come back to her? She was still a maid, in heart and mind. While she was sure that physical attraction played a part in her feelings for Sam, it was not the only reason she wanted him.

She thought of the kiss.

She must admit that, after the recent interlude in his arms, lust played a stronger role than it had a few days ago. So that was what poets wrote about, and why men had fought for Helen at Troy. It was a quite different feeling than she'd had last week. Much more urgent. The feelings were as clear in her mind now as when he had been kissing her. She had but to think for a moment about them to feel the desire renew itself.

It made her feelings for St Aldric all the more unworthy. She had hoped that it would be easier to make the decision between them, once she had talked to Sam. And it certainly was. There would never be anyone in her heart of hearts but Sam Hastings. What she felt for Michael was but a pale imitation.

Why could Sam not understand that?

Aunt Jordan gave up a small yawn and Eve encouraged it with a yawn of her own and a stretch of her arms. She held out the poorly finished shirt for approval. The older woman inspected it and sighed, still disappointed in the work. 'We will try again, next week,' she said. 'And I will be attending the ball at the Merridews tomorrow, as your chaperon.'

'Yes, Aunt Jordan.'

'The duke will be there as well.' Her aunt gave her a significant look. 'It will give you another chance to demonstrate graces that do not come so difficult to you.'

It meant that the time for indecision was nearing an end. He might offer again. If he did, what reason did she have to refuse him? After this afternoon, it was likely that Sam would leave her again before he could learn the truth of his birth. She owed him that, at least.

When her aunt was safely stowed in a carriage and on her way back to her own town house, Eve turned from the door to search out her father. He might have claimed to be intractable this afternoon. But in her experience, even those edicts set in stone could be worn down by begging, pleading and promises to be the best possible daughter, and to never bother him again.

She found him in the study and, as he always did, he looked up from the book he had been reading and smiled as though her interruption was welcome.

'Father?' She smiled to show that the conversation would be a pleasant one and no real disruption. She bent to kiss him on the cheek.

'My dear.' He gave a curious cock of his head, as though already suspecting her intentions. 'Did you have a pleasant evening with your aunt?'

'Of course, Father. She is just gone home,' she said.

'But no visit from the duke this evening,' her father said with a slight frown.

'He was here earlier,' she said, with a little sigh of impatience. She did not wish to discuss Michael. Those conversations always ended with her father hopeful and her searching for a way to postpone capitulation. 'I will see him tomorrow at the Merridews. He cannot spend all his time with me, you know.'

'As long as he was not put off by the presence of another man in the garden with you this morning,' her father said.

'You are speaking of Sam?' She managed an incredulous smile. But she could not very well argue that he was not 'a man'. He had removed any doubts on the subject as he kissed her. 'He is family, Father. And surely it was good to see him after all this time.'

To this, her father responded with a blank look, as though the matter was practically forgotten. 'He has not performed as well as I had hoped. Despite what he says, he hardly needed a university education in the navy.'

'Perhaps he felt the navy needed him,' she suggested. 'He was always an altruist at heart. And I am sure it is better, in the aftermath of a battle, to have a skilled man dealing with the injuries.'

'If that is what makes him happy, then I wish him well.' Her father gave a tired sigh, as though he hoped this concession was sufficient to end the discussion.

'Happy?' she responded with a worried frown. 'Content, perhaps. But to me, he seemed rather unsettled.'

'Because he is no longer comfortable in this house,' her father said. 'He had planned to leave immediately after speaking to me.' He frowned back at her. 'I was surprised to find him still with us when the duke arrived.'

'Because I would not let him go,' Eve said. 'It

is ridiculous for him to stay at an inn when his old room is here and prepared for his return.' She was very close to pouting, which always felt silly, but it had been effective in the past.

'If he showed discontent, perhaps it was your fault for keeping him here.' Her father gave her a candid look. 'There comes a time when one must recognise one's place in society and know when one is intruding.'

'But he was not an intrusion. He belongs here.' Perfectly true, but too insistent. She moderated her tone and held out a supplicating hand. 'He was like a son to you.'

'Like a son is quite different from being a son,' her father reminded her. 'He was my ward. But Sam Hastings is no one's child.'

'Of course he is,' she said. 'Unless you would have me believe that he was hatched from an egg, or some other such fantasy. He came into the world in the usual way, from a union between man and woman.'

'Evelyn! Do not speak of such things. They are unseemly topics for a young lady.'

'I would not have to, if you would be forthcoming with what you know.' She was giving him a full-on pout now, she was sure. She would follow it with tears, if she had to. It was the height of foolishness. But if topics were continually being put off limits to her because of her gender, a reasonable argument would not be possible. And she must have her way.

'Are you going on about that again?' her father said with a sigh. 'Really, Evelyn, you must realize that this is no business of yours.'

'It is my business,' she said and allowed her lip to tremble. Then she pinched the needle prick on her finger, which gave a fresh throb of pain and made her eyes water. 'Because I love and care about…' she paused to gulp back a sob '…both of the men involved.' Let her father think it was not just Sam that she sought to help. She gave him a hopeful smile through the tears. 'St Aldric would be most grateful, I am sure. He has told me often, in candid moments, how sad it is to know that nothing else of his father has survived. He would welcome any family that he might find.'

'It is not up to me to make such decisions,' her

father said a little less confidently. 'I promised, when the boy was merely a baby…'

There. The tears were doing the tick. He was almost ready to admit the truth. 'Any oaths spoken to the old duke can no longer be binding now that both he and his duchess are dead. It is only Michael now. And he is so very alone. If his father had known that telling him would be a mercy, I'm sure he would relieve you from your oath.'

This approach, which did not seem so focused on Sam's happiness, was having its effect. She could see her father's resolve fighting with his desire to impress the duke. 'There are other things that would make St Aldric happy, you know. He will not be alone with a wife and children.'

'He will have those,' she said dismissively.

'When?' her father said, bringing the conversation to a halt. 'You know what he wants, Evie. And what I expect from you. He has waited for months, yet you will not give him an answer.'

'I will, soon,' she said. But perhaps she would not have to. Sam clearly thought himself unworthy. If it was because he lacked money or status, surely it was better to be half-brother to a duke then a barely acknowledged ward.

'Soon, you say? Then I will tell the duke about his brother, at that time.'

'So! You admit the truth, then?' It was hardly a victory if he admitted it to her, but would not tell Sam.

'Yes,' her father said, with another sigh. 'I fulfilled my part of the bargain by seeing to it that the child was educated and launched in a profession. And by keeping my mouth closed, until you came to me, to pry it open.'

'I knew it. I had but to look at them together to be sure.' For a moment, her own triumph overcame all else.

'And now, I suppose, you think you can blurt the story to them at the first opportunity,' her father said, with a disapproving shake of his head.

'I will, if you will not,' she said, stamping her foot like a child.

'And you will hurt them both. If they must be told, as you think they must, it should be done quietly, privately, and by me. It will be shock to both men, even if it is a favourable one. I have documents to show that this is no idle claim and there can be no doubt in the minds of the parties involved.'

He was right. Random assertions by her would mean nothing. She must allow her father to do it in his own time. 'As long as it is done soon,' she said.

'I will do it when you agree to end this nonsense of indecision.' He was looking at her directly, obviously unmoved by her histrionics. 'I have been far too lax with you, Evelyn, and have only myself to blame for this. You are behaving like a spoiled and wilful girl. In all other things I might demur. But in this, I will remain adamant. You are my only child and all that remains of my beloved Sarah. You are my heart and my life. I cannot sleep easy until you are settled. And for you, nothing less than a duke will do.'

So this was the impasse. She had known there would be a day when all the girlish wheedling she could manage would not be enough. And it had finally come. Father would release the truth, if she surrendered her hopes.

She weighed the situation as rationally as she

was able. Both St Aldric and Sam would know their connection. They deserved it. On their last meeting, Sam had made it quite clear that she could wait for ever and never have him. He expected her to marry the duke.

But he had also kissed her, which negated his other behaviour.

She would accept the duke, as her father wished. Betrothed was quite a different thing from married. Many things might happen before they got to the altar.

Then she would write to Sam, tell him of her intentions, and give him one last chance to stop the engagement. If he did nothing, she would go forwards, just as Father wished her to. There were many things right with having Michael as a husband, but only one thing wrong. The fact that she did not love him was hardly an obstacle. She would love only one man in her life. If she could not have him, better to choose someone that she liked.

But everything must be accomplished soon, before Sam took it into his head to leave London for Scotland or the sea. She took a breath, held it for a moment and committed to a plan.

'If you promise that you will tell them both, I will accept St Aldric the very next time he suggests it, which is likely to be tomorrow evening.' Now that she had agreed, it was simply a matter of scheduling and giving Sam a strict timetable in which to change his mind. She glanced at the calendar on the writing desk. 'We shall have an engagement ball next week. The banns will be read starting next Sunday. The ceremony shall follow shortly thereafter. The whole business shall be settled by next month, if that is to your liking. As long as you swear to tell them.'

Her father was looking at her in amazement, as though trying to decide whether to upbraid her for setting standards or show the happiness he felt at getting his way.

'It is all I want for a wedding present from you,' she coaxed. 'And I doubt I would keep the secret for long, now that I have wormed it out of you. I am but a woman, you know.'

He smiled in response to her joke, though she was not being the least bit funny. 'You are probably right. You are a fickle creature, my dear, and I cannot expect you to keep mum. Accept the duke and set a date for the engagement ball. Invite Hastings to it and we shall settle it all on the same night.'

Chapter Seven

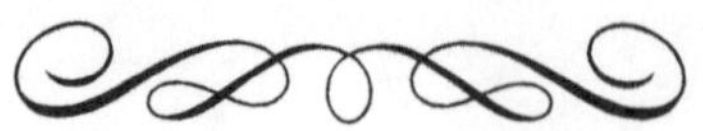

'I do not wish to alarm you, Lady Evelyn, but there is an enormous spider crawling on your shoulder.'

Without thinking, Eve reached to brush it off, realised that she felt no such thing and stopped to stare impolitely at her dance partner.

St Aldric smiled affectionately back at her. 'I have managed to gain your attention at last, have I? A point for me, then. And minus one for you. When faced with such a horror, a young lady is expected to shriek and throw herself into the arms of the nearest gentleman. She is not supposed to settle the matter for herself.'

'I…am sorry.' She tried to remember where they were in the pattern of the dance, so that they could continue without a misstep. She had managed to march through it so far without thinking. But clearly the duke had noticed that he did not have her full attention.

'Is there anything the matter?' he asked.

Yes. Everything. 'No.' She shook her head. 'I am merely distracted.'

'As always, you know to call on me, if there is something I might do to aid you.' He was giving her a surprisingly direct look. Though it was still masked in his characteristic smile, she was sure that he was actively concerned with her and would truly do anything, should she ask.

Let me go. And make Sam love me again. Now there was a request that one did not make of one's future fiancé. Besides, she was not even sure the second half of it was possible.

'Was your visit with your old friend a disappointment?' St Aldric asked, cutting right to the heart of the matter. 'You seem changed since he has come. More sombre.'

'I am sorry,' she repeated, forcing a smile. 'I will try to be more cheerful.'

'Do not change for my sake,' he said. His hand, when next it took hers in the dance, gave hers an encouraging squeeze. 'You cannot help what you feel. But I take it that your Dr Hastings was much altered since you saw him last. That is bound to be disappointing.'

'Yes,' she admitted. Confusing would have been a more accurate way to describe it. There had been nothing disappointing about his kiss.

She glanced at St Aldric, who epitomised disappointment in that particular area. She was being unfair to him. His kisses were as polished and correct as everything else about him. Perhaps it was some flaw in her own character that left her untouched by them.

He continued to smile at her.

She smiled back and felt a wave of the kind of sisterly affection that Sam had tried to thrust upon her, until she had broken his will. This was what it was like, to feel nothing for a man, but to like him well enough not to wish him pain.

'And now that you have seen him, is your mind altered on the subject of our marriage?'

'I...don't understand what you mean.' She tensed and missed a beat, though he corrected easily to compensate for it. The duke had caught her flat footed, again, both in mind and body. She had not expected his next proposal to include any mention of Sam.

His smile was more sympathetic than jolly. 'I am not so dense as all that, Evelyn. You had a *tendre* for the man. I expect you lost your heart to him at a very young age. And that is not an easy thing to forget.'

'You are too perceptive,' she said. 'It is your only fault.' That was not true. He did not miss a beat when they danced. He was never nonplussed or flustered. If perfection was a flaw, he had it in spades.

'I will work to rectify it, once we are married,' he said. 'If you agree to wed me, I shall be as dense as you wish me to be.'

Was he giving her permission to be unfaithful to him? Surely not. But she could not help but think that, when one's heart lay elsewhere, there might be certain advantages to a husband who had announced his willingness to turn a blind eye.

If she had wanted that sort of a marriage, she should be satisfied with the response. But it was likely to destroy the respect she had for him, knowing that he did not care enough for her to be hurt by infidelity.

She thought again of the interlude in Sam's room and tried to focus on the end of it, when he had claimed it nothing more than unworthy lust. On his part, perhaps it had been. But she would have happily died in his arms to give him the peace he requested.

As long as it had occurred after a consummation.

'Will there be any response to my comment? Or are you to keep me guessing?'

'Comment?' She dragged her mind away from Sam and glanced back at the duke again.

'On my willingness to conform to any demands you might set, should you marry me.'

He had made the offer that she had promised to accept and she had been so preoccupied on thoughts of another that she had not heard him. This did not bode well for the future.

'I will offer in another way, if you seek something less businesslike. There could be moonlight, candles and your pick of the jewels in my lock room. I could purchase something new for you, if you do not fancy them. I will get down on one knee. Although I have no experience in it, I will serenade you. Write poetry. I will do anything to see you smile. But you know my feelings on the subject of matrimony. I am eager to hear yours.'

Father was right. She had kept him waiting long enough. If she truly wished to have Sam's approval, it had been given, repeatedly. He proclaimed St Aldric an excellent match. He had also told her, emphatically, that there would be no marriage between the two of them.

Then he had kissed her. Her mind kept coming back to that. She suspected it would, for the rest of her life. Just as she had spent six years thinking of the last kiss, she might spend sixty on this one.

Would the memory of that be enough to sustain her, or would it become a bitter reminder of how a marriage might feel, if it was to the right man?

It did not really matter. Sam had thrust her from the room and was probably still planning to leave the country. And all because she had forced him. If she continued to do so, she would lose his friendship along with his love.

She turned to St Aldric, this time with her full attention, or very near to it. 'I am sorry. I never meant to be cruel to you, or to keep you waiting so long. You are right. It is time that I answered.'

To her surprise, the man at her side looked eager to hear her response. And there was a flicker of doubt in it, as though he was not sure what it might be. She had been so focused on herself and her own wishes that she had been tormenting him with her indifference.

He deserved better.

'Of course I will marry you. At the time of your choosing.'

'A special licence is the thing, I understand,' he said. 'Brides all want them, to show that the groom is ardent and has some pull with court. I will procure one. But the actual ceremony need not be hurried. We must allow enough time to celebrate the event…'

He continued to plan, as eager as a bride, while

Eve retreated to a place where life was simpler, endings happier and kisses as passionate as she knew they could be.

Sam roused to the sound of a knocking at the door. Or perhaps the hammering was in his skull. It was no less than he deserved. Life at sea had inured him to strong drink. But the quantity he had taken in the last day and a half was enough to send a sailor's brain to pounding.

'Doctor Hastings.'

Without another thought he was out of the bed, his hand on his case of medicines. 'What is it? Am I needed?' He shook his head to clear it, ready to face whatever emergency awaited him.

'Nothing so dire, I'm sure. There is a letter for you, sir.' The innkeeper waited nervously in the hall, a liveried footman from Thorne Hall beside him.

Probably a cheerful missive from Evie, expecting him to dance attendance on her, as though nothing had happened between them. But he would not forget the sight of her, kneeling between his thighs.

He shook his head again, harder, and let the pain it caused be a distraction. The girl was far too headstrong for her own good. And naïve as well. The best way to protect that innocence was to stay far away from it. Sam rubbed a hand over his dry eyes. 'Whatever it is, tell him he can take it to the devil.'

The footman looked alarmed, but did not budge. 'I am to put it into your hand directly and wait for an answer, Dr Hastings.' Tom had been an underfootman when Sam had left the Thornes. He had been younger than Evelyn, no more than a child and already in service.

Had she chosen him for this, sure that Sam would remember the boy with sympathy and not wish to give him trouble? She was a demon to torment him with tricks like that. But it was another proof that she knew him as well as he knew himself. He sighed. 'Very well, then.' He held out his hand for the letter. 'Wait.' Then he closed the door on the pair of them and broke the seal.

He could recognise the hand in an instant, for he had seen it often enough, coming to both love and dread her regular letters. It appeared this one could not be avoided. He could not very well climb out a second-storey window in an attempt to get away from it, and by sending Tom she had made it impossible to deny its receipt.

Sam.

He held his breath. The start was innocent enough. But there was not a thing he could stand to hear from the girl, after the shame of what had happened between them.

Firstly, let me apologise for coming to your rooms and upsetting you as I did. I had no right and no invitation.

And no reason to apologise, since the fault and the sin had been totally his.

I must offer a second apology for trying to control the course of your life and choose your future to suit myself. I have no doubt that you are quite capable of surviving without me. It is pure selfishness on my part to try to manage you.

But I beg you, with all my heart, not to return to the sea. Above all, do not go there on my account. I swear, I will do what is necessary to keep you safe, even if that requires me to cease communication with you.

Dear Evie. She was frightened for him and willing to do anything to preserve his unworthy life. He felt the tightness in his chest, half-joy, half-regret, that came with any thought of her. He smoothed the letter in his hands and read more.

On your recommendation, and that of my father, along with the continued requests from the duke himself, I have agreed to St Aldric's offer of marriage. To celebrate the engagement, Father is giving a ball this coming Wednesday. I must remind you, you promised to attend. And despite all that happened after, I hold you to that promise.

Damn the girl. He had promised. And despite what reason demanded, he did not want to go so soon.

If it is truly your wish that I marry, I need your strength to help me carry it through. And if, for any reason, it is not, then you must tell me before that time.

I await your answer...

Et cetera.

For the first time in her life, Evelyn Thorne had done exactly as he'd told her to. It was a trap, of course. She'd finished the letter with a reminder that he might stop the proceedings at any time. He had but to ask and she would cry off.

And in that, she had created the perfect hell for him. It was no less than he deserved, he supposed. He had revealed all to her, or as much as he ever would. Now that she knew he had feelings for her, she sought to inflame them with jealousy. He had given her reason to hope, even as he had pushed her away.

But before that, he had approved her match and promised to attend her wedding. As her older brother, he owed her as much. If he did not want her to think of him, ever again, as anything more than that, he had best learn to play that part.

He went to the table, took up his pen and wrote.

Evie,

You have nothing to apologise for. It is I who am at fault. As to what happened yesterday, it is best that we never speak of it again. I will forget if you shall.

As to my going to sea again? It is clear that this distresses you. My plans are not set. If it is so important to you, I will forgo the navy and practise on land.

But be damned if he would go to work for St Aldric. That was too much to expect of him.

As to your wedding, I am supremely happy for you, and send my congratulations to his Grace as well. I will remain in London and attend your engagement ball and wedding, just as I said. You have my word. Eagerly awaiting the day that I might call you her Grace, instead of my dear little Evie...

He scribbled a signature at the bottom, then blotted and sealed it before opening his door and calling to the footman, who was still waiting in the hall.

There. It was done and the letter was on its way. It might as well have been written on black-bordered mourning stationery, for all the satisfaction he felt. Even though the situation had been hopeless from the first, he could not help feeling a fresh sadness at losing her, any more than he could keep from wanting her.

But in medicine he had found that it was sometimes necessary to give the patient poison to counteract a more serious malady. Attending her wedding would be so to him. Swallowing this bitter pill would be the first step towards a cure for his affliction.

Chapter Eight

Evie was beautiful. Sam had known that already, of course. He had never seen her decked in finery. He had thought her lovely in a simple day frock, but tonight she was magnificent. The silk of her ball gown was as blue as her eyes, and as smooth as her hair. A necklace of gold and diamonds lay, like a collar of stars, about her lovely white throat.

Perhaps Thorne had been right all along. Even without the complication of blood, the creature that stood before him could not have been his. The necklace alone was worth a year's salary. He could never have afforded to put it there. And to her, it was nothing more than her mother's necklace that she had never been old enough to wear. With St Aldric, she would have this and better. A different jewel for every month of the year and a room full of ball gowns to wear them with.

With the duke at her side, the picture was complete. He was tall, handsome and nearly as golden as she. He smiled at her as though it was an honour for him to have won her. They were like two pieces of statuary, designed to complement each other. As a duchess, she would glitter, as she did tonight, from without and within. She was already so bright that it hurt to look upon her.

Yet he could not seem to stop. Once he had fulfilled his promise to her, he would be gone for good. If memories were all he had for sustenance, he would burn each detail into his brain so that he might never forget. As he waited to be presented to the happy couple, he did his best to mask the hunger he felt for her and arrange his face in an expression of brotherly pride.

'Sam.' She reached out and took his hands in hers.

'Evelyn.' She leaned in, presenting her cheek to be kissed. He could not very well avoid it without looking silly. He leaned forwards as well, kissing the air a scant inch from her skin. Even then, his lips tingled as if a spark sizzled between them, bridging the gap.

'It is so good to see you here. I feared you would not come.' She whispered it in his ear as he leaned close to her. When he leaned back, she searched his face with worried eyes. 'It has been almost a week.'

Since he had very nearly ravished her in his rooms. He still woke each night from a dream where the ending to that interlude had been different and he had felt her gasping in passion beneath him. 'I promised I would be here, to celebrate your happiness.'

'That is most kind of you,' St Aldric said. He was still at her side, quietly possessive.

'My felicitations to you as well, your Grace.' He bowed, feeling stiff and awkward.

'Thank you, Doctor.' St Aldric was better at managing a gracious response.

Evie was staring at the pair of them, as though hoping that there could be anything more than cordial dislike between them.

'And now, if you will excuse me?' Sam raised a

genuine smile at the thought of escaping. 'I must not keep you from the other guests.'

There. He was through with the first challenge. Now he must manage a few hours of courtesy and then he could be on his way again. But when Evie was involved, nothing was ever that easy. Was it just because she was the hostess that she seemed to be everywhere he turned? Or was she actually following him through the gathering, showing up where he least expected her, to flash a smile or blow a kiss?

Each time, he turned away, pretending that he did not notice, or had not seen, or was too busy in conversation with another to speak to her. At last she caught him standing alone by the dance floor, with no excuse to avoid her.

'Dance with me.' She was holding out a hand to him, sure he would come to her, as he always had, and swing her easily in his arms.

'I do not think that is wise,' he replied. Just the thought of touching her made his palms begin to sweat.

'Dancing, not wise?' She laughed. 'Is that your professional opinion? I assumed that such harmless exercise would be recommended by a physician.'

'You know that is not what I mean,' he said in a harsh whisper, glancing around to be sure that no one else could hear.

She gave him a coquettish flutter of her fan. 'I really have no idea. If you mean something specific by the refusal, you had best tell me directly.'

'If you truly mean to marry St Aldric, I think it is unwise for the two of us to dance,' he said through gritted teeth.

'My commitment to him has not stopped me from standing up with every other man in this room. Save yourself, of course. You have been avoiding me.'

'I have not,' he said, wishing that it was not such an obvious lie.

'I am sure that St Aldric has no objection to it.'

'What he wishes does not concern me.' And now he sounded like a jealous fool.

'If not him, then whom? What reason could you possibly have that would prevent you? If people notice you avoiding me, they will wonder. And they will talk.'

Now she had trapped him. She was probably right. Someone would remark at how strangely he behaved around her. Above all else, there must be no talk.

She continued to pressure him, sure that he could not refuse. 'I am open for the next waltz. Stand up with me and stop being silly about it.' She gave him a sly smile. 'It will be over before you realise and, I swear, no harm shall come to you.'

'No! Not a waltz.' He'd said it too loudly and a matron a few feet away gave him a sharp, disapproving look. But the idea was simply too much to bear. 'I will stand up with you, if you insist. But let it be some other dance.'

'All right,' she said, giving him a disgusted sigh. 'La Belle Assembly. It is starting now. And we will stand up with St Aldric and another, so you need have no fear of upsetting him.'

Sam's eyes narrowed. 'It is not from fear of him that I refuse you.'

'Fear of me, then?' She gave a toss of her head. 'That does little to improve my opinion of you.'

The letter had been a lie. She did not need

moral support to make this decision. She merely wished another opportunity to torment him. He seized her hand with no real gentleness, as he had done when they were children, and dragged her towards the centre of the room. 'Come on, then, brat. The sooner it is begun, the sooner it will be done. Then you must leave me in peace for the rest of the night.'

He had been right. This had been a mistake.

She had thought that a public temptation might force a commitment out of him. At the very least, it would give her one last chance to be with him. But this was not the memory she wished for. It was too painful.

They shared the set with St Aldric and his partner, a lady of great beauty and little wit, but she was a skilled dancer and little more was required of her now. They traded bows and curtsies, and the dance began.

Sam swung her to a place opposite him and circled. And though he followed the steps to the letter, it felt as though she was being stalked by a wolf. In comparison, St Aldric's pass was easy, relaxed and confident. He smiled at her, enjoying the dance, enjoying her company.

She turned back to Sam, who was watching her too intently, a frown upon his face. His eyes bored into hers, taking in her every movement to the point where it became alarming. And past the frown and the beetled brow, she saw the truth.

Jealousy. Frustration. Rage. It was not distaste that kept him away. He wanted her as much as he had on the day that they had kissed.

And now she danced with St Aldric again. In his eyes, she saw nothing of importance. He possessed her already, or very nearly did, and thus he was thinking of something else.

But each time Sam took her hand, it was as if he never meant to let it go. The release was stiff and graceless, as though he'd forced his fingers open to let her escape. He was gritting his teeth in concentration. He did not need to count the steps, for he seemed to have no trouble keeping track. His posture was rigid, as though he suffered pain at each touch of her fingers.

Yet he could not seem to get enough of it.

When they finished, she allowed him to escort

her back to the place they had been standing. Then he walked away without a word.

She stood for a moment, in indecision, then she followed, out of the ballroom and through the halls of the house, to the place she knew he must go.

It was dark in the garden, smelling of night-blooming flowers and the beginnings of the still heat that would drive the *ton* to Bath or the country. They had not bothered to light the yard, so no one had strayed from the house. But someone who was familiar with it would need no light to find the garden bench under the elm. He was there, of course, a dim outline against the darker bark of the tree.

She sat down beside him. He did not acknowledge her presence, so they sat in silence for a time, not wanting to spoil the moment. Then he said, 'You promised, Evie. You promised that it would not come to this if I stayed.'

'You were right, before, when you said we could not waltz.' If they had, she'd have made a fool of herself, clinging to him on the dance floor. If she was in his arms, how could she do else?

He sighed. 'You feel it as well, then? I hoped perhaps you had been spared and that the other day, in my rooms, had been an aberration.'

She nodded, wondering if he could see. 'If it is not possible to master the feeling, then perhaps we should not try.'

He did not move to look at her, sitting as still as he had when she'd joined him. 'You do not understand. Not truly.'

'I understand that there are scant minutes left, before my choice is irrevocable. If there is any reason to change my mind, I will take it.' She reached for his hand and squeezed it, hoping that he would feel the urgency.

'You must trust me to know what is best for you,' he said with his best physician's tone, 'And I tell you that there is no reason for you not to marry St Aldric. In fact, I insist that you do.'

'Why must you keep playing the tiresome older brother?' she said with an amazed shake of the head.

'I have not donc it enough in recent years.' he replied. 'You need someone to talk some sense into you, since your father cannot seem to manage it.'

'Sometimes, I wonder if you are just thick, despite all your fancy education, or if you are joking with me. You know that brotherly wisdom is not what I want from you.'

'What else can I offer?' He sounded so hopeless, she wavered between pity and annoyance. It seemed that if she wanted words of love, she would have to speak them herself.

'Let me put it plainly, since you refuse to. I love you, Sam. I always will. I wish you to offer for me. But you are pretending that you do not understand. Please, Sam. Please. Declare yourself. I will speak to Michael, and to Father.' She gave his hand another urgent squeeze.

She shifted her body, ever so slightly, towards his and turned so that their faces were only inches apart—and suddenly they were kissing in a moonlit garden. In an instant, it was as it had been in his rooms.

She tried to remember where she was. And when. There were people waiting for her in the ballroom. And a man who wanted nothing more than to make her his bride.

But she could not stop wanting the man who would make no promises. There were so many things wrong with the moment that she could hardly enumerate them.

So she thought of none of them and opened her mouth.

She could hear the rustle of her own satin gown as he crushed her body to his and feel the rapid flutter of her tongue in his mouth. His circled to still it, filling her mouth with the taste of him.

His hand was at the back of her neck and he hesitated, stroking once, carefully, so as not to disarrange the curls. Then he smoothed over her neck, her shoulders, her throat, and very carefully slipped inside the bodice of her gown.

The man she loved was touching her breast. She caught her breath and held it, giving him more room to touch her as he kissed. His hand was gentle, even as his mouth was not, warm on her skin, his fingertips barely touching the puckering tip as his teeth grazed her lips and his tongue pushed deep, retreated and returned.

If this was what he wanted from her, she would gladly give it. Her legs trembled and her centre was wet, as she knew it would be when the time was right to join with a man. If she had the nerve to touch him, as she had in his room, she was sure that he would be hard for her and just as eager as she felt.

Her hands were beneath his coat, on his waist. It was improper, but wonderful. She slipped them under the bottom of his waistcoat and could almost feel his ribs through the linen of his shirt.

In response, his fingers closed on her nipple and tugged. She gasped, biting at his lower lip, wanting more. He must give it to her. He simply must. She needed his tongue on her breast, and his body in hers, so that they might be one in flesh, as they had always been in spirit.

Her hands dropped lower, clutching him firmly by the backside. And she pulled herself upwards, forwards, into his lap. And for just a moment, she felt the bulge of him pressing against her through her gown. The trembling seemed to come from inside her now, like the expectant rumbling at the beginning of a storm.

He pulled himself away from the kiss and whispered into her ear. 'Is this what you want from me?' He thrust his hips against her.

She nodded eagerly, digging her fingers into the muscles of his body and pressing herself against the hardness, praying that this was the answer he wanted, the one that would make him continue.

'Because it is what I want from you,' he said. The hand that caressed her breasts squeezed to the point of pain. 'It is what I have wanted from you since my first desire. To taste your body with my mouth. To push myself into you. To spill my seed.'

'Yes,' she whispered, closing her eyes. 'Yes. Yes.' She could imagine him there and the moment of helpless surrender when she became his.

'This is what I want,' he whispered, his breath in her ear even hotter than his kiss. 'And it has nothing to do with a romantic declaration, or a marriage. I want to have you, right now, here in the garden, naked like Eve. I want to use you for my pleasure, without a thought to what is right or good.'

He was making something that would be

wonderful sound sordid. But she wanted it all the same.

The hand that had been at her waist pressed her head to his mouth so that he might continue to whisper, 'I want your body, Evie. That is all. I want to ruin you. I want what I want. I do not care if it destroys us both. That is why I left you six years ago. And that is why I must leave now.'

And then he pushed her away, out of his lap and on to her side of the bench. The night air had grown cold. She could feel it against her exposed breasts and the constriction of the bodice pulled low under them.

'Compose yourself. And then go back into the house and find your betrothed.' His voice was as cold as the air, passionless. 'As I have told you before, I am not the man for you. Marry St Aldric, Evie. Please. He will care for you. I cannot. But you must stop this pointless hoping that there will ever be another choice.' He stood then and walked away. Deeper into the garden or back into the house? She was not sure.

She tugged the bodice back into place and laid a hand against her cheek, waiting for the blush to subside. If she sat here a while longer, she would be as cold as he was, but not as emotionless. She was angry.

Sam Hastings was all she had ever wanted. She had tricked him into coming here and followed him like a fool, only to be refused again. He had brought her to the brink of fulfilment. And then he'd delivered nothing more than threats and speeches, like some Drury Lane villain.

Did he not realise that she might have taken some pleasure in the act that he found so base and unworthy? Her body still seethed with desire. It was as if she was waiting for some gift that only Sam could give her. He had shown it to her, held it close and then snatched it away at the last minute. Then he behaved as though she was the one who was cruel.

Well, it would not happen again. Tonight, she would make her choice once and for all. She would go to another man and would never turn back. At least St Aldric would not reject her without even trying to love her.

She would tell herself that what she felt for Sam had been a childish infatuation. And now, as he claimed, it was nothing more than lust. Neither of those things had a place in her future. She would leave the memories of the good Dr Hastings in the nursery where they belonged.

And some day she would revisit the memory of this night and find it as brittle and faded as a dried flower. She would look at her children, hers and Michael's. And she would wonder why she had ever been so silly as to want another man.

But not today. Today it would be difficult. She thought of St Aldric and his many good qualities. And, slowly, she felt the ardour subside. Michael was handsome. He was kind. He had an excellent sense of humour. When he saw her, he would walk towards her, not away. And there would be a smile on his face that showed promise and a joyful anticipation of their future together.

She stood and took a breath. The air was clean and cool, and if it smelled of a man's cologne, it was probably just her imagination. Then she straightened her dress and went back to the house.

Chapter Nine

'Lady Evelyn has made me the happiest man in London.'

Sam had returned to the ballroom in time to see the announcement. St Aldric was grinning like an idiot, oblivious to the fact that the woman beside him was still flushed from the kisses Sam had given her.

As he had for so much of his life, he stood by mute, struggling with his own base desires, and allowed it to happen. He had stood in the garden for a time, waiting to see that Evie got back to the house without help. There were no tears from her, no passionate cries that he return. A profound silence seemed to emanate from the spot they had been. A few minutes later, she had got up and walked away from him.

It felt like the day he had first put out to sea and watched England retreating until it was a dot on the horizon. He had seen the water as nothing more than distance between him and the woman he could not help but love. It was the same now. The ballroom seemed to stretch before him as couples filled the dance floor for a waltz. And Sam was on the only solid spot, losing her all over again.

He took a sip of his drink, wishing that it was something stronger. Another hour, perhaps, and he could make his excuses and depart. But he did not have to stand here, watching her be happy without him.

It had been so easy in the garden, when all innocent, brotherly thoughts had fled like animals before an advancing fire. She wanted him. He must have her, or he would go mad. He felt the pressure building, the desperation to drag her to the ground, throw up her skirts and lose himself in the softness of her body.

He imagined entering, in one quick thrust, the tightness of her, the rush. Her cry of shock at the loss of her maidenhead.

And discovery. Thorne's shout of outrage. The discovery of the truth.

Disgusting. Obscene. Profane.

He'd pushed her away, horrified at what he had done, but secretly, sinfully triumphant. She was his in all ways that mattered. She would marry the duke. But each time he touched her, she would be thinking of this moment and how much she had wanted another.

It must never happen again. He would go to the Americas this time. Or Jamaica. With luck he would succumb to a fever and his suffering would end.

He turned away from the crowd, hoping to find diversion, in cards, brandy or perhaps a pretty face that might distract him from the only woman he really cared to look at.

Instead, he found their father.

'Doctor Hendricks.' Lord Thorne had tracked him in the crowd of well-wishers and Sam checked the height of his raised glass, the fullness of his smile, searching for any telltale signs in his person or behaviour that might show him to be less than enthusiastic for the match.

'Sam.' Now Thorne's tone was as it had been, when he had still been a favoured son. Before he had made his stammering offer for Evie.

'My lord,' he said, with a half-smile that he hoped was not too strained.

'St Aldric and Evelyn have nearly finished their dance. There is no reason to wait longer.'

For what? he wondered. Was he expected to depart already?

But it seemed Thorne was speaking more to himself, than to Sam, as though there was some duty that he had been delaying. 'I…we…wish to speak to you, in my study.' If anything, Thorne looked as uncomfortable as Sam felt. It was odd that he could not match his mood to the festivities. Surely, this must be a moment of triumph.

'Of course, my lord.' Sam glanced at the clock. 'On the half-hour, perhaps? That should give enough time for the crowd to settle.'

'Twenty minutes.' Thorne seemed to see this as some sort of reprieve. 'An excellent idea. Until then.' He moved off through the crowd again and Sam watched him absently accepting congratulations for his daughter's successful match.

It was damned odd.

And there in the centre of the dance floor was Evie. Dear, sweet Evie, looking almost as overwhelmed as Thorne. As she spun past him, in the arms of the duke, her eye caught his, if only for a moment. She gave him a smile of triumph, her eyes shining not with tears but with an almost evil glee. She had done what he'd requested. She hoped he was satisfied.

If he must lose her—not that she had ever been his—it was better that it be this way. She was angry with him and would be so for some time. If she had doubts about this decision, he would be gone before she expressed them.

But all there proclaimed St Aldric an exemplary man, truly a golden child, who had not allowed the ease of his success to taint his innate goodness. He was worthy of Evie. And he obviously adored her. He would treat her as she deserved to be treated. Sam doubted he could ever bring himself to like the duke. But he would have no cause to see the man again, so it did not matter.

The dance ended. And the precious St Aldric

was not at her side, damn him. He had won. The least he could do was enjoy his prize. But Sam had seen Thorne part the couple as soon as the music stopped, whispering something to the duke.

Evelyn had watched. And though she would not have been able to hear what was said, she nodded. There was the strangest look upon her lovely face, as though she was remembering some troublesome detail that rendered the moment less than sweet. Then she had turned back to the crowd, perfection again.

Something was afoot. But damned if Sam could imagine what it might be. The clock ticked out the minutes until his appointment.

When the requisite time has passed, he made his way up the stairs to find Thorne.

And here was St Aldric as well, waiting in the office of his mentor, looking almost like an errant schoolboy, although he had no reason to. The self-deprecation was all the more annoying in its effectiveness. Had he been any other man, Sam would have been instantly in sympathy with him.

But he was not just any man. And Sam could manage nothing more than the expected courtesies. He smiled and bowed to the peer, and to Thorne. 'My lord. Your Grace.'

'Sam.' And there was the old familiarity from Thorne again. Sam greeted it with a cynical smile. Now that Evelyn's fate was sealed, he was to be a favoured son again? Not bloody likely.

'I suppose you are wondering…you are both wondering…why I have asked you here,' Thorne said, unsure which man to look at first. 'It is at Evelyn's behest,' he said.

There was another awkward pause. 'She realised the truth, you see. And has convinced me that, if it was obvious to her, it might be to others. She thinks that perhaps it would be kinder to settle the matter, before there was any speculation. And since you would be here, tonight…'

Then he paused again, as though the previous statements might mean something and need no addition.

St Aldric was looking back with a crooked grin, as though he could not quite contain his amusement. 'As it stands, Thorne, the only speculation occurring is between the two of us. It is clear that you wish to share some information and that it is coming difficult for you. Please, speak. Doctor Hastings and I are quite in the dark.'

Thorne looked back and forth between the two of them now, like a rabbit caught between two foxes. 'I must first say that I mean no disrespect to you, your Grace, or to your father, who was a dear friend of mine. Nor was it ever my wish to betray his confidence.'

'Since he has been dead nearly ten years, he is unlikely to call you out on it,' St Aldric said, with an encouraging smile. 'But I take it that he swore you to some secret or other and that it is weighing heavily on you, now?'

'It is nothing so very serious,' Thorne said, encouragingly. 'Nothing that many other men have not done. There was no real disgrace in it. And you must know that your father was always the worthiest of men.'

'It pleases me to think so,' St Aldric said with a nod.

'It is only because the truth is likely to come

forth with or without my help, that I am speaking now,' Thorne said.

'Then out with it, man,' St Aldric said, with another smile. 'The good doctor can attest that, when pulling a splinter, there is no point in drawing slowly. It only prolongs the pain, as this prolongs suspense. What is this not-so-terribly-dark truth that you have been concealing from the world?'

'This happened when you were just an infant, obviously. And your mother still quite fragile. There was…' another dramatic pause '…an indiscretion.'

Sam's attention had begun to wander. It was clear that, whatever the problem might be, it was St Aldric's concern and not his. Perhaps he was here in case the shock proved too great and a physician was needed. If that was the case, he would have done better to bring his bag.

But there was nothing about the duke that made him think the man would be prone to fits at receiving bad news. His colour was high, of course. But considering the reason for the evening, it was only natural.

'Since both my mother and father are gone from this planet, I see no reason that such information should be concealed any longer. Speak with my blessing. Immediately, in fact.' Even a saint had limited patience. It appeared that St Aldric had reached the end of his.

'There was issue, from this indiscretion,' Throne said hurriedly. 'The child survived. A boy.'

'But that would mean…' St Aldric gave a surprised shake of his head. 'I have a brother?'

'A half-brother,' Thorne said hurriedly.

St Aldric was forwards in an instant, gripping the man's arm. And for the first time since meeting him, Sam saw what he must look like when angry. 'You knew of this? And did not tell me? Damn it, man, I must know all.' He calmed himself just as quickly. But it was clear that he was eager for more news. 'Did my father reveal anything about him? For I would like to know him. No. I must.'

'It will not affect the succession,' Thorne said hurriedly. 'You are the elder. And he is a bastard.'

'I do not care,' St Aldric insisted. 'He is my

blood, whoever he is. He is both kin and responsibility to me. He will not want. I shall be sure if it. I have a brother.' His face split into a grin of amazement.

As usual, St Aldric was proving himself to be the most admirable of men, showing not an ounce of jealousy or outrage at this sudden revelation. There was no sign that he viewed it as an embarrassment. To be gifted with a bastard brother was not an inconvenience to him. On the contrary, he seemed to think it a marvel. Despite his charmed life, the duke had lacked but one thing: a family. And, of course, God had granted him that. Now he was complete.

It was just one more depressing sign that he was the perfect mate for Evie. The man was as kind and generous in private as he was in public. Sam supposed that it was just another sign of his debased character that he still wanted to choke the life from the fellow.

'He has not wanted. Not for a moment,' Thorne said hurriedly. 'Your father put him in my care from the first and swore me to secrecy.' Now he looked past the duke, to Sam. 'I raised him as my own. I told him nothing of his actual parentage. I misled him…'

And now both men in the room were looking at Sam, Thorne giving a shrug of apology.

'I do not understand.' But, of course, he did. This meeting had been about him, all along.

'I did not get you from a foundling home,' Thorne said. 'Your mother was a seamstress named Polly Hastings, who lived in the village of St Aldric. She was struck with childbed fever and could not care for you. I took you away, shortly before she died.'

'My mother.' He'd known he had one, of course. But he had not thought of her in years. And his father…

'You told me…' He could not manage to finish the sentence, for the implications of it, though they had been horrible before, were becoming all too clear.

'What I told you before does not matter,' Thorne said in warning, as though he would be likely to blurt out the story he had been told, in all its repellent detail. 'This is the truth: the old duke was your father.'

And that changed everything. In one sentence, he had gone from monster to man. His desires were neither base nor sinful. They were a perfectly natural affection towards the most beautiful of women. There was no impediment to realising them.

The room was spinning. Or perhaps he was. The sudden lightness of spirit might have set him turning like a windmill. It had certainly unsettled his brain. His tongue was stuck to the roof of his mouth. He could not seem to call for the brandy he so desperately needed. Or the air, which he could not manage to take into his lungs.

When Sam opened his eyes again, he was staring at the ceiling. Thank God, Evie had not been in the room to witness this or she'd have teased him 'til his dying day. It was bad enough to have fainted in the presence of St Aldric and Thorne. There was no point in arguing that he had weathered battle without incident. He had been ankle deep in blood and severed limbs, the screams of the wounded and the smell of death close about him, and had never had such a reaction as this.

They must think him weak, easily overwrought, sensitive and emotional.

But it was worse to think of Evie standing over him, laughing at his discomfiture, while the man who was his half-brother weathered this news with good humour and *sang-froid*.

'Are you all right?' St Aldric was looking down at him with a bemused expression that split into another grin. An oddly familiar expression, for it was rather like the one that Sam saw when shaving. Now that he was encouraged to see the similarities, it was plain that they were brothers. Colouring, eyes, the height of the forehead and position of the ears—all were similar to his. There could be no doubting it.

The Duke held out a hand, ignoring his silence. 'I suppose this comes as rather a shock.'

'You have no idea.' It had been the rush of knowledge that had done for him, just now, the new facts pushing the old certainties from his head. And the knowledge that he had been wrong, so very wrong, about the one thing he had been most sure of.

Evie could never be his. She was his sister. His

feelings for her, no matter how powerful, were vile and fetid. All his adult life, he had known himself for a sick dog, or a base sinner, unworthy of the company of the one he most wanted. No amount of distance, violence or Bible thumbing had offered relief.

Then, in an instant, he had been washed clean. The well-manicured hand still hovered before him, blurring slightly as the last of the swoon cleared itself and his pulse returned to normal. Sam gripped it and allowed himself to be pulled upright.

'It was a great shock to me as well,' St Aldric supplied, trying to put him at ease. 'I had grown quite used to the fact that I was the last leaf on a dead family tree.'

'I am a natural son,' Sam said, still confused by the man's joy at this news. 'I hardly think that counts me as part of your tree. A weed beside it, perhaps.'

'Better that than blasted, bare ground.' St Aldric was staring at him with a strange hunger, then pulled him forwards into a brotherly hug.

Sam felt the hand that had lifted him clapping

him firmly on the back, then the duke gripped him by the shoulders and held him apart, staring into his face as Sam had to the other, a moment ago. St Aldric was memorising the features, cataloguing, comparing, finding the agreements just as Sam had done and nodding in revelation. 'You have no idea what a relief it is to find kin of any kind, when one has resigned oneself to being alone.'

There was no response Sam could offer to this but a blank stare. He had never felt the need of a brother and certainly did not want the father and sister that he'd thought he had. It was better, so much better, to think oneself alone than to have those. Now, he had been thrown into yet another family that he did not wish for.

His feelings must have shown on his face, for St Aldric looked away in embarrassment. 'I am sorry. I did not think. You know all too well what it is like to be alone. But that has changed for both of us. I will acknowledge you, of course. And I will help you in any way I can. I'd have done it for Evelyn's sake, of course. But there is so much more reason now.'

Evie.

He had forgotten the events of the past hour. Lady Evelyn Thorne was now engaged to the Duke of St Aldric, who was, apparently, his brother. It was like losing her, only to think he had won her, and then lose her again. Everything had been settled between the three of them. It would be most unworthy of Sam to spoil the happiness of his brother and steal Evie's best chance at a match.

The decision took little more than an instant to make. It might be unworthy, but he would do it in a heartbeat. Evie loved him. Her words and actions had proved it, just an hour ago. Sam owed nothing to this interloper. Despite what St Aldric might think, they were still enemies. All the good will and kittens in the world did not change the fact.

'As I said when we first met in the garden, your help will not be required,' Sam said, softly.

St Aldric's eyes widened in surprise, as though he had never considered the possibility that someone might refuse him. 'What reason would you have to deny me? Surely I can open doors for you that you could not open yourself.'

'I have been content with making my own way thus far,' Sam reminded him.

'Sam.' Thorne's voice held a fatherly warning to mind his manners and accept the charity of his betters. It gave him an hysterical desire to laugh in the man's face. There was no earthly reason he need follow the advice. Thorne might have raised him, but the pretences were so false as to render the relationship without value.

'And now you might be more than content,' St Aldric said. 'You must be my personal physician, as Evelyn suggested. It would be little more than an honorary position for many years, I assure you. I am young and healthy. But there would be a stipend attached to it. And the honour of association. You are still unmarried. I suspect that there would be many women who would actively seek you out.'

'Evie.' He was struck dumb yet again, and, if he was not careful, he would faint for the second time in his life, right here on the office carpet.

'And you said she knows of this already?' St

Aldric looked to Thorne for confirmation. 'It makes her actions so much clearer. The eagerness that we meet. The suggestion that I take you on.' St Aldric was grinning at him again. 'For a time, I quite thought that there was something else to it. But now it is clear. You will be as a double brother to her. And dear to both of us.'

If St Aldric had his way, Sam would be just as separate as he had always been from the one woman he wanted and forced for ever into her company. 'You presume far too much, your Grace.' He pulled away from the man who held him and shook the wrinkles from his coat as a distraction from the thoughts racing in his head.

'You are an ungrateful brat, Sam.' After what he had done, Thorne seemed to think he had a right to an opinion.

Sam turned his anger on the more deserving target. 'You have no right to lecture me on it, now that the truth is out. What are you to me, sir, after all this time?'

'Only the man who raised you,' Thorne said.

'And fed me on lies like they were mother's milk,' Sam snapped back. 'For Evie's sake, we will not discuss the extent of your perfidy. But do not think I forgive you for it.'

Thorne's eyes widened. 'She is my only child. I did what was best for her and for you as well.'

From the other side of the room, Sam heard a soft clearing of a throat and remembered that they were not alone with the argument. He turned back towards the duke and stared at the man in silence. Did St Aldric really think it was an honour to be so abandoned by one's father that one had no identity at all? Then Sam had been wrong about him. The man was a fool.

'I can see that it will take some time for us to get used to the knowledge that has been imparted, and to digest the change and decide what best to do about it,' St Aldric said, still the soul of diplomacy. It was clear that he did not think himself in need of delay, but he meant to hold his tongue and bide his time for the sake of his brother. He reached out a hand and patted Thorne upon the back. 'Thank you, for my father and myself, for the service you have done my family and for revealing it to us now.' They were the right words for the circumstance and it made Sam feel all the smaller for his petulance, no matter how justified it might have been. 'And now, if you gentlemen will excuse me?' He gave a gracious nod as though he had already heard the affirmative response and excused himself from the room.

Thorne stared at Sam and let out a hiss of disapproval. 'You might be the son of a duke, Hastings, but it is clear that you have inherited none of that family's grace. Evelyn was right to choose St Aldric over you, for you are behaving just as I assumed you would.'

'Thank you for confirming that,' Sam said.

'Her happiness has been all that mattered, to me, from the first. And you were never meant to be a part of that.' Thorne was smiling in triumph, like a priest in the throes of religious mania. 'Go ahead. Run to her. Tell her everything. Try to turn her against me. See if she thanks you for it.'

Evie looked at her father with the adoration of an only daughter. In her eyes, he could do no wrong. To hear otherwise would crush her. Sam shook his head. 'No, Thorne. I do not think so.

I would have to be willing to break Evie's heart and claim it is for her own good. The day I do that is the day I prove I am truly your son.'

Chapter Ten

After leaving Thorne, Sam still wanted a drink. In a case like this, Dr Hastings would prescribe a brandy for shock. That and a chance to sit down and sort this through without people prying through the contents of his head. 'Physician, heal thyself,' he muttered and headed towards the decanter in the library.

When his nerves were settled, he would find Evie. He must apologise for his words in the garden. As soon as they had cleared the air of that, he could persuade her to cry off on the engagement and come away with him. She had offered once to run to Gretna with him. It would have to do. There was no time for a proper courtship and banns.

He must get her out of London before the scandal broke. And, even more important, he must get her away from this house. He had been able to manage a chilly respect when he'd believed Thorne was his father. But he owed that man nothing at all now. He had not been taken in out of love or charity, or for any bond of family. His presence here had been to curry favour with old St Aldric. It was nothing more than that. It was only a matter of time before he shouted those words in Thorne's face, along with the ugliness that Sam had believed to be the truth.

Evie must never know of that. Thorne had been trying, in his own sick way, to protect her. If Sam was to be her husband, that task would fall to him. And he would make a better job of it.

'Hastings!'

Sam flinched. His newfound brother had been waiting for him in the hall, eager to continue the conversation. He turned stiffly. 'Your Grace.'

St Aldric looked faintly amused. 'You cannot avoid me for the rest of your life, you know. Not if I mean to claim you as family.'

Perhaps not. But he was tempted to try. 'I am

not avoiding you,' he said cautiously. 'I thought you meant to let things settle, before talking again.'

'How long is that likely to take?' St Aldric asked. Apparently, he thought a few moments were long enough to re-order one's whole understanding of life.

'It was a considerable shock to me, to learn the truth after all this time.'

St Aldric nodded. 'I suppose I cannot really imagine, any more than you could imagine my life.'

'My presence or absence could not really matter so much to it,' Sam said, drily.

The duke seemed surprised. 'On the contrary. Although I can afford almost any luxury, this was one thing that I knew to be ever out of my reach. One cannot purchase a brother.'

Any more than one could cease to have a sister. But it had just happened to Sam. He looked at the duke again, trying to raise some of the filial emotion that the man hoped for. He felt only jealousy. 'It takes more than blood to create such a link.'

'Perhaps,' the duke allowed. 'But I see no reason why the two of us might not at least become friends.'

If he saw no reason, he was deliberately being obtuse. But then, when they had met, the duke had assumed a bond existed between Sam and Evie. Sam had denied it and relinquished all claim on her. He could not suddenly reverse the position without explaining his reasons.

He did not want to become like Thorne, willing to say anything to achieve his ends. The shame of his earlier beliefs would die quietly, assuming he did not speak of them to all and sundry. Newfound kinship did not entitle St Aldric to every sordid detail of Sam's past.

In his mind, he transferred the cordial indifference he had shared with Thorne to his new family and gave a respectful nod. 'I am sorry. You are correct. I am being unreasonable about the situation.'

'As you said, it was a shock,' the duke reminded him. 'You can hardly be expected to take it calmly. Your temper does not offend me in the least. Certain latitudes of personality are permitted. In families.' The words made him grin again, showing that he felt no reservations at all in the discovery. It was yet another example of the man's superior nature.

And it was tiresome in the extreme. 'All the same, I apologise,' Sam said, grudgingly.

'Apology accepted,' said the duke. There was no corresponding apology, of course, because the man never did anything to need one. He was, as he had been from the first, perfect.

But now he was engaged to Evelyn.

'Now that we have settled that, you must excuse me,' Sam said, suddenly sure that if he had to look into the handsome face and listen to one more sensible word he would fall on the duke like an animal and beat him senseless.

'A moment.' St Aldric held up a single finger, as though such a small gesture was all he needed to subdue Sam. 'This still does not answer my question. I do not see any reason why we cannot become friends. Do you?'

It was an opportunity to be honest, for once.

To explain the situation and how impossible a friendship between them would be.

Instead, he lied through his teeth. 'Of course not.'

'Then it is settled.' The duke was smiling at him as though a few words had cemented their relationship. 'If you wish, I will put you forth as a member of my club.'

Where they could keep running into each other, he supposed. Did the man intend to be omnipresent in his life?

St Aldric saw his hesitation. 'It will give you a chance to meet other gentlemen and advance to the position of your choosing. You might not wish to be my personal physician. But there are any number of gouty old lords in need of your services. Perhaps one of them would suit you.'

When put this way, it was actually tempting. And he'd have been on it like a shot had the offer come from any other person. Sam felt a moment's wistfulness for the family he might have had, had things been different. He'd not thought he needed an actual father. At least not for affection. But a hand on his shoulder to steady him, educate him and introduce him in the correct circles would have been damned helpful.

He'd had it once from Thorne. That man had proved false in the end. Then he remembered the reason for Thorne's change of heart. It was the same reason he could not accept the help of the man in front of him. Evelyn.

Sam gave a respectful nod of his head, trying to keep the sarcasm from his voice. 'Thank you for your offer, your Grace. But, regretfully, I decline. I doubt I would have much use for a club membership, for I have no intention of remaining in the city.' Nor would he be particularly welcome there, should his plans come to fruition. He would either leave alone a broken man, or scuttle the romantic hopes of the very man who sought to help him.

'Very well, then. As you wish.' By the look on his face St Aldric could not decide whether to be angry or disappointed by this latest rejection, probably because he was not used to hearing the word no. 'But you must dine with me tomorrow night. I insist upon it.'

Insisted, did he? And what did that have to do

with Sam's own desires? He searched for the first available lie. 'Unfortunately, that will not be possible. I am otherwise engaged. Now, if you will please excuse me?' Then he made his retreat to find the only person he really wanted to see.

'Evelyn. We must speak.' Sam was striding towards her with a grim smile on his face and all the purpose and conviction of the British navy.

Eve felt a flutter of apprehension. It seemed she had been holding her breath for the better part of an hour, waiting for some word from the office. Perhaps she would see the two of them, side by side, shaking hands and revelling in their good fortune. It would be awkward, for a while. But maybe some good would come of the evening and she would feel less guilty for her lapse in the garden.

But the duke was nowhere to be seen. And Sam was using her full name, as he only did when he was angry, or maintaining the same artificial formality that he had been.

'Sam.' She turned to him, reminding herself that she must not reach for his hands, or give any of the other familiar gestures that seemed to inflame his passion for her.

He ignored her coldness and held her by the shoulders. Unlike the gentle touches in the garden, his grip was tight, as though he feared she would run from him if he released her. 'How long have you known?'

There could be no question of what he meant. And it did not seem that the truth had set him free, as the Bible said. He looked more guarded than ever. She looked away, afraid to meet his eyes. Must she feel guilty for this as well? It was the one thing she had been sure of.

Other than her love for Sam, of course. And that had been wrong. Now, she was losing confidence in this decision as well. 'I have suspected for some time. When St Aldric began spending time with me at the beginning of the Season, he seemed so familiar to me, like an old friend, though I knew I had not met him before. But it was only a suspicion. And then you returned and I knew.'

'Why did you not come to me with this information? Or did you tell him?' His voice was as rough as his hands and the words were punctuated by a shake.

'Sam!' She pulled away from him. 'Do not think that our old friendship allows you to treat me so. I did not tell you because I had no proof. You would have thought the idea ridiculous and dismissed it. As for telling St Aldric…'

Now it was his turn to look away. Was he still jealous? Why did he bother to show it now, when it was too late? 'It was unworthy of me to accuse you. Just now, he was as surprised as I.'

'I did not mean to keep a secret from either of you. It was only recently that I took my suspicions to Father and more recently still that I convinced him to admit the truth and share the news with you and Michael.'

'Your fiancé,' Sam said, looking seriously at her.

'Your brother,' she added, wishing that he could be happy about the news.

'And was the decision to marry in any way tied to this revelation? The timing seems most convenient.'

'Father agreed to share the information, now

that Michael is to be my husband,' she said. And what difference could that make to anything?

'Then this marriage—' Sam gave a broad sweep of his hand '—has nothing to do with the depth of your affection for St Aldric.'

Why did he wait until now to care about how she felt about St Aldric? He had not troubled to ask her of this before. Then, he had been set on her accepting the man, ordering her about, as if he had right to. 'He is as good a man as one could hope for. You told me so yourself. When you know him better, you will like him, as I do.'

'That is quite impossible, Evie. And you should know the reason why.'

Her patience was at an end. 'Do not blame me for a separation between the two of you. You made it quite clear that you did not want to marry me. You spoke highly of him. You insisted that I must accept him. I did as you asked. Put aside your petty jealousy and make peace with the results. Now that I have made my decision, the rivalry is over between you.'

'That's what you think, is it?' He was looking at her with a crooked, rather cold smile, as though he was a frustrated schoolmaster with a particularly dense student. 'Enough of him, then. We will talk no more about it. Tell me more about your feelings for me.' He had been practically trembling with his, just a few hours before. But the news had changed him. Now he was resolute, guarded and very much in control.

'My feelings?' She was not even sure what to call them. How was she to tell him?

His hands turned gentle, settling on the exposed skin between gown and gloves. 'You said you loved me, tonight, before the announcement.'

'Before the announcement,' she repeated. That was more important than the words that came before. 'What I said then no longer matters,' she said, pulling free of his hands again.

'It does to me. Tell me again.' His voice was low, coaxing and unlike any tone he had used before. She felt it under her skin, burning into her very heart. It was the voice she had longed to hear, from the first moment he had returned. The boy who'd left had finally come back to claim her.

She had to fight to remember why she must not listen to him. 'I am engaged to St Aldric now.'

'And you love him?' Sam tipped his head to the side and gave her the kind of expectant look she was used to, when he wished to wheedle some truth out of her. It made her feel like a little girl again.

Now, of all times, after she had chosen to do the adult thing and put nonsense aside, it was infuriating to be treated as a child. 'What I feel for St Aldric is none of your business.'

'But what you feel for me is.' His fingers tightened on her arm again and she felt herself melt.

'Let me go.' The words did not sound very convincing, even to her.

'I tried,' he said, in a tired voice. 'And I was wrong to do so. I find it is not possible.'

'And yet you agreed to do it, not once, but many times over the last week.' How many chances had she been expected to give him to declare his feelings? And he had denied them every time.

'I lied. But you must have known that, for you kept badgering me to change my mind.' He was smiling now, as though secure in his ability to break her down. He was pulling her closer.

She pulled away, trying to resist him. Did he

not understand the sacrifice she had made? And all because he would not admit to his feelings when he'd had the chance. Then she reminded herself that accepting St Aldric was not a sacrifice. It was a triumph. 'If you think you can have me now, after a few romantic speeches, you are sorely mistaken, Sam Hastings.'

'Am I?' His smile had changed, full of a knowing confidence that both frightened and excited her. 'Let us see, shall we?' And with one last tug she was in his arms.

This kiss was different than the others had been and, as she surrendered to it, she wondered if he had an infinite variety of tricks to use on her. Perhaps he did. Everything about this kiss shouted, *I know you. I know what you want.*

How was that possible, when she was not even sure of it herself? He opened her mouth with his tongue and explored with an innate confidence, claiming each inch of it for himself. When he'd finished, she was breathless, as though her heart had forgotten to beat while she was in his arms.

'Very well,' he said, with another confident smile. 'I will not concern myself with your feelings for any other man. I think we have proved them to be insignificant.' His finger was tracing along the cord of her neck.

She batted it away. 'It is too late for this.'

But he paused for only a moment before returning to his teasing. 'The moon is full, and we are alone,' he reminded her. 'And in love. I cannot think of a better time.'

The correct response would be *I do not love you. Leave me alone.* But it would have been a lie so great that she could not get her lips to form the words. Instead, she repeated, 'You are a day too late.'

'As long as we both breathe, there is time,' he said, pulling her into his arms again. His hands were on her waist, possessively smoothing over the ribs, and he was kissing her again, his lips travelling from her mouth to her shoulder. There was no anger in him, as there had been when he had complained of his inability to master himself. It was no selfish attempt to use her. This was a calculated attempt to arouse her. 'Come with me, Evie,' he whispered. 'To the garden. I want to show you something.'

This was the Sam that she remembered, always daring her to be reckless.

But the girl he'd left was gone. She had banished her tonight and vowed to be different. There would be no more visits to the garden, no dabbling in medicine, no more nonsense and foolishness.

Evie Thorne might have allowed these kisses and encouraged this man to pull her down into the grass and do what he would with her. But the future Duchess of St Aldric must not.

She yanked her arm out of Sam's grip, pulled back and let fly with a slap that was worthy of any she'd dealt him as a child, the sort that had sent him to Father over the unfairness of a gender that would taunt him unmercifully while knowing he could not strike back.

He pulled away from her, hand on his cheek, shocked and angry.

'I said *no*.' She hardly recognised her own voice. It sounded low, powerful and humourless. It was the voice of a woman, not a girl. It was a voice to be obeyed. She stared him down, unflinching, and watched the anger change to wariness.

'Evie?' he said, with a wry smile.

'I think it best that you refer to me as Lady Evelyn,' she said. 'As you have been doing since your return. You will take no more liberties with me, in public or in private. In turn, I will be polite and respectful, for Michael's sake. But if you cannot abide these terms, our previous connection will not matter, nor your kinship with the duke. You will not be welcome in my home and in public I shall cut you dead.' Aunt Jordan would have been proud of the speech. It was just as it should have been, when one had given offence to this degree.

But the look on Sam's face was heartbreaking. At least she would have the satisfaction of knowing that she had been right in bringing forth the truth. The careworn look that had troubled her was gone from his face, but now he was staring at her as though he could not quite believe what he was hearing. He rubbed his jaw, feeling the tenderness where she had slapped him. 'Why, Lady Evelyn, I do believe that you are serious.'

'Of course I am serious, you cloth-headed dolt.'

It was a weak epithet that harkened back to the time when they were children. The words that suited him now—rake, seducer, villain—were ones she could not manage to say, even if they were true. 'Unless you can manage to treat me with respect, there can be no more contact between us.'

'Because you are betrothed to St Aldric.' And now he looked as though he wanted to laugh.

'Yes,' she said, in frustration. Had she been wrong about him all along? Was her oldest friend and first love really so cruel as to mock her for behaving exactly as she should have from the first?

'Very well, then.' He was agreeing, but he continued to smile as though caught in some enormous joke. 'I will treat you as I ought, with respect. But not because of your precious Michael. I will do it so that you may see how empty simple courtesy is, compared to our true feelings for each other.' He reached out a single finger and touched her cheek.

And she swore she could feel every touch he

had given her in the garden and taste his kiss on her lips.

'In a week, you will be begging me to take you away from him. And I will have mercy on you and do it. I have fought battles to resist you that render your engagement to the duke insignificant. And I have lost every one of them. We belong together, Evie. For better or worse.'

Chapter Eleven

Sam entered the duke's London home with the sort of grim resignation he saved for delivering bad news to patients. He had received the invitation with indifference and refused it out of hand. But after his talk with Evie, he reconsidered. She would likely be attending as well. Since she did not intend to see him alone, he had best take any opportunity offered to be in the same room with her.

And perhaps a small show of co-operation on his part would sate St Aldric's desire to know him better. He had stopped Sam again, before his exit from the Thorne home, to renew his offers of aid, advancement or at the very least a good meal. It appeared that the duke meant to badger him non-stop until he had made a brother of him.

Sam could halt such efforts in their tracks by announcing that his plans to seduce the man's fiancée would make friendship difficult, but such honesty was more likely to reduce his contact with Evie than increase it. He had always thought himself a moral man, other than the repellent desire to bed his own sister, which put him square on the road to damnation. But now that his love was proved innocent, it appeared that he was capable of covetousness, duplicity and any number of other vices, if it helped him gain her back.

He would not hurt her, of course. But he would not have to. It would take only the smallest of nudges and she would drop the plan to marry another, and come running back into his arms. Then things would finally be as they had been meant to be, from the first.

Tonight, she was playing right into his hands. The duke must have informed Evie of Sam's reticence. This morning, he'd another visit from Tom the footman and a terse note from Evie, reminding him of his promise to help her with this match. Unless Sam wanted to make the breach between them plain to St Aldric and answer the questions that would follow, he must put on a smile, come to dinner and prove that he had accepted the new boundaries of their friendship.

He had jotted down a hurried answer. The fact that she had set boundaries did not mean that he must be contained by them. When he had encouraged her to marry, he had not been in full possession of the facts.

When he had realised that he could offer no other explanation than that, he had ripped the paper to bits. Some things must wait until they were alone and face to face. Perhaps, by then, he would have come up with a better answer than this, for it sounded weak, even to him.

Instead, he had written a single line of assent to her and another to St Aldric. He would go to dinner and make nice, as long as it suited him to do so. If an opportunity presented itself to further his plans for Evie, he would take it and boundaries be damned.

But now, he was rethinking his plan. His first impression on arrival at St Aldric's home, was that his rival had him hopelessly outgunned. The house where their father had lived was magnificent. Everything about it was larger, more ornate and superior to the Thorne town house. The ceilings were higher, the carpets deeper and the furniture glowed with a patina of age and privilege. There were likely several other properties even larger, scattered about the country.

Sam thought back for a moment to the little cabin in the bulkhead of the *Matilda*, with its brass fittings and worn wood desk. He had been quite proud of it. It was a symbol of that most cherished thing aboard ships, privacy. To have one's own space was a luxury.

But this house was full: of people, of servants, of responsibility. Was the duke ever truly alone? If not, then Sam would not envy him. Nor would Sam envy him for Evie, who, despite what *The Times* might say, would never truly belong to St Aldric. She loved Sam. And he had no reason not to love her back.

Nearly four-and-twenty hours later, that fact still took him unawares and brought a smile to his face. The identity of his father and his connection to this great house were incidental, compared to the broken link to Lord Thorne. He was free to love Evie. There was justice in the world, after all.

'Welcome.' St Aldric was striding out into the hall to meet him, as though he did not trust the butler to deliver Sam the last few feet to the place where guests were gathering for the meal. 'I am pleased that you managed to break your other engagement and attend. I hope it did not cause difficulty.'

'Not at all,' Sam said. They both knew he had lied. But if the duke wished to pretend it had been true, then so would he.

Now the great man sat at the head of the table, and a fine table it was. The silver was heavy and the knives so sharp he might have performed surgery with them. The crystal was delicate and the wines superb. The linen under it all was whiter than Sam had ever seen, and monogrammed at the corner with the family crest.

His family crest, Sam thought distantly. *And mine.* If St Aldric still wanted to claim him, when all was said and done, there might be advantages to allying himself with his true father's house. They would not outweigh his love for Evelyn, of course. Until she cried off, he and St Aldric were at war.

But if they battled tonight, at least it would be in good company. Along with Evie and her father, there was a bishop, a cabinet minister and his wife, and several young ladies and gentlemen of excellent breeding and manners.

Seated next to him was Lady Caroline…something or other. It did him no credit that he was thinking of Evie during the introduction and now could not remember the woman's name. St Aldric had given him a significant look, as though assuring him that this was an excellent match, should he pursue it.

As if the girl would want anything to do with him. Or he her. He could choose his own wife. In fact, he had made his choice already, though he doubted that St Aldric would approve of it.

Evie was giving no outward sign that she remembered their last meeting. She was too smart to think that he would give her up without a fight, but apparently she awaited his next move. She treated him with courtesy and charm, just as she did the other guests. She was as glittering as the ring on her hand and as gracious as a duchess, listening attentively to the conversation around her, contributing intelligently and hanging on every word that the duke spoke.

And damn the man if he was not worth listening to. He was polite, witty and intelligent. He responded to debate with a cool rationality that won the point more often than it lost. He did not allow his head to be clouded by his own rank and people's instinctive deference to it.

Worst of all, he had announced to the others at the gathering that there was a connection between them. He told all who would listen that Sam was a 'distinguished physician' and that they 'shared a father.' He acted as though the sudden appearance of a bastard brother was the best imaginable news.

It was maddening. What could Sam possibly say that could distinguish himself to Evie? And now St Aldric was questioning him about his profession, making an effort to draw him into the conversation and phrasing questions so that Sam could display his skill without seeming boastful.

It was artfully done. He'd have been most grateful if he hadn't already hated the man. There was no way to bring him down a notch, nor could Sam think of a way to raise himself in the eyes of his beloved. And then, as did all conversations that touched on medicine and care, someone enquired about poor Princess Charlotte.

Inwardly, he flinched. It was a doctor's worst nightmare to be put in care of a beloved member of the royal family, only to manage the birth so badly as to lose both the patient and the unborn child. His usual plan was to have as little opinion as possible, so as not to offend. But then, in a flash of insight, he saw the direction the conversation would likely go, if he but let it alone. 'I would not dare to make a judgement without being in the room for the birth. There can frequently be complications that are not apparent until labor has begun. But I think the subsequent suicide of the attending physician speaks for how deeply he felt.'

'He should not have been involved at all,' Evelyn said, with no attempt at diplomacy.

Sam was eager to see what would happen next.

It had been so long since he'd shared one, he'd forgotten that a dinner with Evie was often more diverting than a night at the theatre. It had been less than twenty-four hours since the engagement. And at less than a day, her plan to be a suitable wife to St Aldric had lasted longer than he'd have wagered.

Her blunt statement caused the rest of the table to fall silent in shock. While ladies no doubt had an opinion about such things, they certainly did not voice them with such candour in mixed company. But Evie was not just any lady, thought Sam, and did his best to hide his smile. She had a smattering of medical training and strong feelings on the subject of obstetrics.

'And who would you recommend be at her side at such a time,' St Aldric asked, 'if not a trusted family physician?' The smile he gave her was more indulgent than critical and more patient than many men would be.

But Evie would see nothing but the criticism. 'I suspect a midwife would have done just as well,' she said, chin up in a posture that Sam recognised as a warning sign that she was prepared to fight all who might disagree.

St Aldric continued to smile at her, but glanced at Sam as though expecting an ally. 'It appears that my betrothed does not think much of your profession.'

Evie saved Sam the trouble of choosing a side by answering for herself. 'It is not that I think less of Dr Hastings, or doctors in general. It is simply that I disagree with any man's ability to fully understand birth and labor.'

'They train at university, study texts and the work of experienced physicians,' argued St Aldric. 'I am sure they must learn sufficiently.'

'Most texts are written by men. I doubt their competence in a process that they themselves cannot experience,' Evie said solemnly.

Her future husband could not help himself. He laughed out loud.

For a moment, Sam felt sympathy with his new-found brother. The poor fellow could not have picked a better way to get on his beloved's wrong side.

'Furthermore,' she announced over the sound

of the duke's mirth, 'we would still have our dear princess, if the doctors had not been so ham-handed in their treatment of her.'

It was quite possible that this was the case. It was not Sam's place to question the practice of other doctors. He'd have come to the defence of his profession had it been any other evening. To-night, he did not wish to cross Evie by disagreeing. The high road was diplomatic silence.

But St Aldric was not aware of that. 'What can you possibly know of such things, Evelyn? You are but a maid, after all.' It was an honest question, but it sounded almost like he was questioning her virtue.

It was like watching a man dig his own grave.

Sam saw the increasingly mutinous glint in her eyes as she readied her argument. 'I have been present at any number of deliveries when we are in the country,' she announced. 'I have also read the texts that they use at university. In comparison, I studied the techniques of the village midwives and aided them in their work. They now deem me so proficient that I can manage all but the most difficult deliveries before calling for a doctor.'

Around the table there were giggles and gasps. The good Lady Caroline blushed and the bishop on her other side blanched white.

Just as he remembered her, Evie was unaffected by approval or disapproval. When she was truly set in a course, she would not be moved. Her animosity forgotten, she looked to Sam as though conferring with a colleague. 'I would not attempt a Caesarean, of course. But neither would you, I wager, unless you were sure that there was little to no hope that the mother would be alive to see the birth.'

'They seldom survive the operation,' he agreed. 'But perhaps at table is not the best place—'

'From what I understand, the physician in residence bled Princess Charlotte for months and starved her instead of feeding her up stout. Then he left her to labor for days without so much as ergot to hurry things along.'

As a physician, he could not contradict what she said. She did not argue from ignorance on the subject. She had explored the techniques of both physician and midwife. He had been trained in only one and taught to ignore the other as inferior.

'And the baby was breech. If the lady's hips are small it is like trying to force a melon through a keyhole.'

There a genteel squeak from one of the more impressionable ladies and a soft moan from Lord Thorne.

'He did not use the forceps when he had the chance,' she finished.

'I thought you did not believe in such things,' Sam supplied helpfully and waited for the fun to continue.

'She should not even know what they are,' St Aldric announced, trying to regain control of the conversation.

Evie ignored him. 'I said they were used too often. Not that they were totally useless,' she said. 'Although if you are skilled, it is possible to turn the child without them.'

'Is she in the habit of discussing such things with you?' St Aldric demanded of Sam, going a bit white around the mouth. Sam wondered if he was still so eager to have a doctor in the family. He suspected that, when they had a chance to speak in private, he would be called to task for leading Evelyn astray.

He took a sip of his wine. 'I have not been in the country for years, your Grace. But Lady Evelyn has questioned me at length on the subject of medicine, since I have been home.' Let the man think what he would of that. If he did not understand the risk of another man spending so much time with his future wife, then he deserved to lose her.

'Is that what you talk about?' St Aldric seemed honestly surprised at this. Had he expected the worst? And if so, why did he do nothing to prevent it?

'We talk of other things as well, Michael,' Evelyn said dismissively, totally ignorant of the duke's jealousy.

'You should not be talking of this under any circumstances,' the bishop announced, no longer able to contain himself. 'Nor should you doubt the superiority of men in all things, or worry overlong about alleviating the suffering of the childbed. It is woman's lot, since the fall of Eve.'

'But men are not superior in all things at all times,' Evelyn said with a smile. 'And my sympathies to my biblical namesake, but do you seriously believe that the Lord made women to suffer and then invented opiates to taunt us with the possibility of relief? I believe the Bible also says something about being stewards to the land. I assume that means that we are to make use of such natural palliatives when we find them.'

Now her father was holding his head, as though he were experiencing a megrim. The lady at his side gave a little shriek of outrage. But the matron opposite Lord Thorne responded with a solemn nod of approval.

'Evelyn.' There was the faintest touch of warning in the duke's tone, as though he thought that he could manage the sort of unspoken communication that one sometimes saw in couples whose hearts were beating in time.

'Yes, Michael?' Evie responded with a sweetness that would have had a smart man diving under the table for protection.

'Do you think it is proper to disagree with a gentleman who is our guest?'

Evie blinked back at him, all innocence again. 'Only on such subjects where I am sure he is wrong.'

The bishop tossed his napkin aside and pushed away from the table. 'You must excuse me, your Grace. But this is simply too much.' He stood and stormed from the room.

St Aldric's ability to maintain decorum was dependent on a certain level of respect and the polite co-operation of all present. But Sam could have warned him that, with Evie involved, he would never see it again. Now the normally composed duke was trapped on the horns of a dilemma. Did he discipline his betrothed at the dinner table? Mollify his guests? Pronounce her opinions charming and pretend that nothing had happened?

After a moment's cogitation, he muttered, 'Bloody hell', and threw his napkin aside as well. Then he rose with a smile, added, 'Ladies and gentlemen, if you will excuse me for a moment', and disappeared after the clergyman.

At his rising, the people around the table dutifully came to their feet and settled back into their chairs when it was clear that he would not stay long enough to notice.

A nervous silence fell over the remaining guests, who began to eat quickly, as though hoping for an excuse to end the evening early. Sam savoured the remaining courses in his own good time. He could not remember a better meal.

'Evelyn, may I speak to you in the library for a moment?'

'Of course, Michael.' The other guests had already departed and her father paused nervously in the doorway, his hat in his hand.

The duke gave him a reassuring smile. 'You needn't wait, Lord Thorne. If you wish, you might return home and send the carriage back for Evelyn. She will be perfectly safe here for an hour or so.'

Her father gave a relieved nod and abandoned her to her fate. Although Eve could not imagine that it was anything too grim. She watched Michael closely as he led her to the library and saw no reason to fear. He was clearly annoyed, but not so angry as to frown. A few kisses and a small amount of contrition on her part, and life would continue as normal.

Or perhaps more than a few kisses. Now that they were engaged, there was no reason that she could not employ more drastic methods to distract him, should he prove difficult. They would be alone for at least an hour and some of that time might be spent in the first real intimacy she had shared with Michael.

As he closed the door behind them, he looked at her in surprise. 'You needn't be afraid, Evelyn. I am not happy with what occurred at dinner, but I am not going to be such an ogre as to deserve the look you are giving me.' He sat on the sofa by the fire and gestured to the cushion at his side.

'What look?' She glanced at herself in the mirror above the mantel. *Oh, dear.* It was one thing to appear penitent and quite another to look like Joan of Arc on the way to the stake. And she had not even been thinking about her behaviour. She had been thinking of being alone with Michael.

She turned back to him, quickly composing

her expression to something more pleasant, and took her seat. 'I am sorry, Michael, for the Friday face and my behaviour earlier.'

'I am pleased to hear you say so,' he said. Perhaps that was all that was required of her.

'Of course, the conversation at dinner could not be helped,' she added, so that he might understand her better.

'On the contrary,' he said softly, 'I think it can.'

'I fail to see how,' she replied. 'It is not as if I can sit silent through the meal.'

But judging by the look Michael was giving her, that was precisely what he expected her to do. 'There will be situations in the future that require you to exercise restraint.'

'Even when the opinions are as wrong-headed as some that were expressed this evening?'

'Especially then,' he said with a nod.

'I fear that will be impossible,' she said, again. 'I have many strong opinions of my own.

'But when we are married, I expect you to have fewer of them,' he said. 'And at dinner, it would be better to limit yourself to discussion of the food, or the weather, or perhaps fashion.' He smiled as though the matter was now quite settled.

And then he kissed her.

The interlude that followed was frustrating. She did not particularly want to be kissed until the discussion between them had been settled in her favour. She understood full well what he was doing, since she had considered using just such a technique to win him over. Her mouth was occupied. Therefore she could not argue with him. It was manipulation, pure and simple.

And it did not seem to be working. His lips were on her shoulder and his hands on her ribs. While she no longer felt like talking, she was far too clear headed for this to be going as he'd hoped. If it had been Sam, she would have been near to losing her senses by now.

And she would have been kissing him back. The half-hearted attempt she was making to show affection to Michael would be attributed to innocence, for a while at least. But what happened if her uninterest continued to the wedding night and after?

* * *

After a half an hour or so, Michael released her. It appeared that he was not bothered by her lack of enthusiasm. His breathing was fast, his skin flushed and his eyes more black than blue. 'For the sake of your reputation, I must stop now,' he said, brushing back a lock of her hair. 'But I will see you again, tomorrow. Your father wishes me to stay to dinner. And after…' He kissed her again, more ardently.

Or so she suspected. It felt no different to her.

Then he escorted her out into the hall and helped her with her wrap, seeing her safely to the waiting carriage.

The door has scarcely shut before she realised that she was not alone. She peered into the darkness on the opposite bench. 'Sam?'

'So I am no longer Dr Hastings to you?'

She had spoken out of habit, forgetting her plan of the previous evening. 'Whatever I might call you, you owe me an explanation for this intrusion.'

He eased himself into the light from the carriage lamp and shrugged. 'I saw your carriage and asked Maddoc, the coachman, if he might drop me at the inn on your way home. There is nothing more than that.'

'The carriage has gone and come once already tonight. Why did you not ride with my father?'

He shrugged again. 'I prefer to ride with you.'

'And so you waited outside in the dark for the better part of an hour?'

He leaned forwards, hands on knees to look at her, his apathy dissipating under her scepticism. 'Very well, then. The truth. I wished to talk to you about the dinner.'

'The duke has already lectured me,' she said, 'If that's what you mean to do, you needn't bother.'

'He has kissed you as well,' Sam said. 'I suppose you do not wish me to do that, either.'

'Certainly not,' she said. 'And what makes you think such horrid things about me?'

'You find kissing him to be horrid?' he said, cheered. 'Then I shan't fear a comparison between us.'

'I do not,' she said. The recent interlude had been more forgettable than horrid. 'I mean, why must you assume that we kissed?'

'Because he had you all to himself for some time. A little dining-room drama would not prevent him from seizing the moment.' He smiled in a knowing way that made her body tingle. 'And because I know what you look like when you have been kissed.'

'Then you waylaid me to remind me of something I would prefer to forget.' She thought for a minute. 'And by that, I mean your kisses. Do not think to attempt it again, or I shall scream for the coachman.'

'That is what Lady Evelyn would do,' he said. 'But the woman I love would be more likely to hit me than cry for help.'

'Striking a gentleman is probably another thing that Michael would not approve of,' she said. 'If you are a gentleman, that is. Of late, you do not behave like one.'

He ignored the insult. 'So the Saint does not approve of you.'

'He said no such thing,' she replied. 'He merely wishes that I be more circumspect,' But that was not how it had seemed. Michael had tried to put a muzzle on her and then tried to kiss away the feelings of confinement.

Sam noticed her silence. 'For what it is worth, I saw nothing wrong with you speaking out. Your argument was well reasoned. The bishop's was not.' Then he turned serious. 'You are an intelligent woman, Evie. You have strong feelings about many things. Never be afraid to give voice to them. Those of us who truly love you do not want that to change.'

'Thank you,' she said. That, at least, had not altered between them. He understood her, even if she did not understand her own feelings. But such understanding would be useless, if he withdrew from her life and let her husband take that place. It was as it should be. But that did not mean she could not grieve the loss.

'I was wrong to tell you to marry him,' Sam said, suddenly. 'You two do not suit.'

He was right, but she had known that when she'd made her promise to Michael. 'You are saying this to trick me into your arms.'

He shook his head. 'I am saying it because it is true. You will not make each other happy.'

'We will not make each other unhappy.' Not intentionally, at least.

'That is not enough,' he said. 'You deserve so much more.'

'Than to marry a saint?' she said.

'You deserve your freedom. And you will be forced to give that up, if you marry St Aldric.'

'You can't know that.' But, of course, he could. Wealth and power did not come without responsibilities. She had tricked herself into believing that St Aldric would be the one to shoulder those. But after tonight, it was clear that he meant her to carry her share.

'If you were mine, you would have an equal say in our future.' The idea was almost as seductive as his kisses.

She must not listen to it. 'You say that now. But you have changed your tune before.'

'Not about my chosen profession,' he said. 'Believe what you like about my feelings for you. But when have you ever heard me lie about that? I am sorry to admit it, but I loved medicine long before I loved you. It is to me as St Aldric's title is to him: an unchangeable part of myself. If you marry me, you will have my head as well as my heart. And I will teach you anything you ask.'

And what would she use the knowledge for? At dinner, it had not just been St Aldric she'd upset. The people around her had been horrified. Her father had been ashamed. 'After tonight, I think we have both seen where my curiosity has got me. I am already dancing at the edge of polite society. And now you are come with an offer to make me worse.'

'I offer to let you be yourself,' he said. 'And that is something that St Aldric would never allow. When you are ready to admit the truth, Evie, come to me. I will be waiting.'

The horses were slowing. Sam swung easily to his feet before they had stopped and was out the door with a thank you to the coachman, and not another word to her.

Chapter Twelve

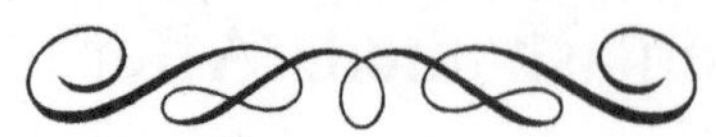

'Doctor Hastings.' Whoever it was did not think the incessant knocking on his door would be enough. A ray of light from the hall struck Sam, rousing him halfway from sleep, and the sound of his name did the rest. But he could not seem to bring himself to full wakefulness. For a moment, he was back aboard ship and it was the cabin boy come for him. Only an emergency brought a visit at this hour.

'Ehh?'

Not a cabin boy this time. Tom the footman, who looked just as uncomfortable about waking him as he had in delivering Evie's letter, but this time he stood his ground without shifting and almost quivered with the need to act quickly.

'Evelyn?' Sam was fully awake now. A day

had passed, and there had been no response to his offers in the carriage. But if she had decided to accept him, the hour did not matter.

'No, sir. It is the duke. He wishes to see you immediately.'

'Tell him to go to the devil.' Perhaps St Aldric could not read the hands on the clock. But the last thing Sam needed, at this hour, was another strained conversation with his new brother. 'Whatever it is, it can wait until morning.'

'That would not be wise, Mr Hastings. Doctor Hastings,' Tom corrected. 'He said it was a professional matter and of some importance. He called me to his room, but would not allow me to enter. He said I must not wake any but you and that I must bring you immediately.'

And much as he might wish to, there was no way to avoid the call, if it was truly a medical matter. He was bound by oath to go to the man. 'If this is but a bit of sleeplessness caused by overindulgence, I shall not be happy about it.' But what right did he have to take it out on this scared rabbit of a footman? Tom had even less choice than he when faced with such a summons.

'He seemed most distressed,' Tom said weakly. 'Please, sir.'

'Give me a moment, then, to gather my bag and pull on some clothes. And leave the candle.'

'Yes, Doctor.' The footman put his taper on the table and closed the door again.

Sam put on breeches, dragged a coat over his nightshirt and pulled on some boots. If it truly was an emergency, he could not waste the time for more. Then he blew out the light and fumbled his way to the hall and the waiting servant.

Tom led him down to the street and the Thorne carriage, helping him to a seat.

'Is the duke visiting, then?'

'Yes, sir. He came to dinner, but could not finish it. He did not feel well enough to return home. We put him in the blue room.' Tom closed the door and hopped on the back as the driver set off at a smart pace for Evelyn's home.

When they arrived, Sam was taken to the back entrance and through the kitchen, so that his arrival would disturb as little of the household as possible. Once on the servants' steps, he needed no guidance to find the guest suite. Things had not changed here since he was a boy.

He rapped once, quietly, on the door of the duke's room and waited, listening.

'Enter,' the voice that answered rasped, but whether it was from illness or an effort to keep quiet, Sam was not sure. He pushed through the unlocked door, holding his candle above his head to cast light on the patient.

St Aldric was sitting on the edge of his bed, legs dangling and head hung, as though it was almost too great an effort to hold it on his shoulders. 'I am sorry to wake you. But something is very wrong with me,' he croaked.

The symptoms developing were so obvious that Sam could guess the disease without stepping into the room. If the diagnosis he suspected was accurate, the situation was likely to get worse before it got better. 'You were right to call me and not to alarm the house. May I have your permission to examine you, your Grace?'

The duke gave a shallow laugh. 'At your service, Doctor.'

Sam lit the other candles in the room and stirred

the fire, for the duke shivered, even though the room was warm. Then he set the candle he had brought in the holder on the bedside table and laid a hand across the duke's forehead.

Feverish. And how long had this been coming? He'd been in high colour almost two days ago, after the ball. Had his hand been warm that day, when it had touched him? Probably not, for Sam had noticed nothing at dinner the previous evening.

He pulled the little tube from his bag and explained, 'This is a recent invention. I will use it to listen to your heart and lungs.'

'Dead handy thing,' the duke said, showing a weak interest. 'It is good to know that you are an innovator.'

Sam pulled the duke's nightshirt aside and listened. His heart seemed rather fast, though his lungs were not congested. The tempo was probably due to nerves. But the swellings at the jaw line were plainly beginning. The duke's normally handsome face looked like a squirrel in fall with nut-packed cheeks. Sam ran a practised hand over the duke's glands and felt him flinch.

'Tender?' he asked. 'From here, towards the ears?'

'Yes.' The response could not disguise the pain.

'How about your belly?' Sam gave a few quick prods in the area by the pancreas and saw the duke flinch again. The infection was taking to his organs? This was not good. Not good at all.

He raised the hem of the nightshirt and looked lower. 'Pain in the testes?'

'Some,' the duke admitted.

How to explain this, so that the man was not overly alarmed? Sam gave his most sage, calming nod.

The duke looked at him as many patients did, as though hoping they would be told that it was nothing, and that they should stop being a ninny and go back to bed. 'You know what it is?'

And so did he, most likely. He merely wished for a different answer. 'A contagious inflammation of the glands, normally found in children. More serious in adults, however.' Particularly in men. But the duke was likely to know that, soon enough.

'Fatal?' the duke asked, after a slight hesitation.

'Hardly,' Sam said with what he hoped was a reassuring smile. 'Uncomfortable, of course. We must keep you isolated, both for your own sake and to keep you from transmitting the disease to others.'

'I cannot. Parliament…' The duke made to rise from the bed.

Sam put a firm hand on the middle of his chest and pushed him back. 'It will be quite beyond you for some weeks.'

'Evelyn…' the duke said, as though remembering that he must also be concerned for her. She would never have been second in his mind, had St Aldric truly loved her.

'She has already had this disease. In childhood, when it was less severe.' Sam could remember it distinctly, for he had been sick at the same time. 'Since she is immune, she will be able to visit you, if you wish it. But others had best keep their distance.'

'I notice you are not afraid for your health.'

'A physician is hardly useful, if he fears the diseases he treats,' Sam said. 'And I have a particularly strong constitution.'

'You must get it from your mother, then,' St Aldric said, with another groan. 'Our father was taken with all manner of illnesses. And now, look at me.'

'One disease is hardly a sign of a weak constitution,' Sam reminded him, 'and this is a common one. I am surprised you have not had it before.'

'You would know better than I,' St Aldric said. 'All I was sure of is that I needed a doctor.' He looked hopefully at Sam. 'I know you have refused my offers of a place in my household. But would you be willing to treat me now?'

'Of course,' Sam said, surprised that the question would even arise. 'You are in need of me.'

'So it is the position I offered that you disliked and not me specifically,' the duke said, his eyes narrowing in the puffy face. 'I had begun to suspect it was otherwise.'

'My feelings and the reasons behind them are not of importance at the moment,' Sam said briskly, fumbling in his bag to be sure that he was well stocked in the necessary medications. 'Do not trouble yourself about them. To me, you are no different than any other patient.' He removed the tinctures of opium and belladonna and set them on the bedside table. 'Right now, we must work to get you well and to prevent the spread of the disease to others in the household. Might you have any idea where you acquired the malady? How long have you been feeling poorly?'

'Several days, at least,' the duke muttered. 'And I did visit the sick ward in the foundling hospital where I am a patron. Some of the children there were ill.'

Sam all but snorted in disgust. If he had been called out of bed to treat any other duke, he would have found that the man had lain with a poxy whore, or was troubled by gout. But the Saint had got mumps from caring for orphaned children. It seemed that Sam could have no scrap of moral superiority, even in the privacy of his own mind.

He took care not to be sarcastic when he answered. 'That is the likely source. I can use the date to guess at the duration of the contagion. With luck, most of the household has already suffered through this. But to be safe, we will empty this floor and keep visits from servants to a minimum.'

The duke touched his own cheek, feeling the lumps on either side. 'I would just as soon stay out of sight, so as not to cause alarm.'

Sam searched his swollen face for any sign of vanity, then concluded that the truth was no different from the words. The man did not want to cause fuss or bother by infecting others or frightening the maids. Humble as well as charitable. St Aldric was infinitely tedious in his virtue.

'Think of it less as an absence of bother and more as a quarantine,' Sam said firmly, reaching for the glass at the bedside and measuring drops of medicine from the two bottles into the water. 'When Lord Thorne awakes I shall have him inform the rest of the house. And I will give you an opiate to help you sleep. I am sorry to say that the discomfort is likely to increase before it abates. But the belladonna should help with that. Meals for the next few days will be soft and rather bland.'

The duke sighed. 'The way I feel, I do not think I will care to eat them, so it will suit me well.' He took the cup and drained it in one gulp and settled back into the pillows. 'Send my apologies to Evelyn and to Lord Thorne for the inconvenience.'

As if Thorne would care, as long as the duke was alive. He would deem it an honour to have the man under his roof for a fortnight, whatever his condition. 'Of course, your Grace. I will visit you again in the morning.' Unable to stop himself, he gave a respectful bow of his head, took up his candle again and then withdrew to leave the patient to sleep.

Standing in the hall, Sam weighed his options. If it had been a normal patient, he'd have woken the housekeeper and left her the medicine and instructions to find him should conditions change. There was really little to do, other than to watch the man suffer through it and help him to deal with any consequences that the disease left behind.

But this was no mere mortal. He was treating a duke. Even if it had not been the Saint, Sam would have insisted on staying in the house, so that he might meet the man's every need. It would be a waste of his time. But it would be expected by all involved.

And it was not just any duke. It was his own brother. As family, he was probably expected to worry. Sam could manage no feelings beyond concern that St Aldric would be in the same house as Evelyn for at least a fortnight. He would be in no mood for romance.

But with her interest in medicine, Evie would be a dutiful nurse and very sympathetic. She would station herself at the bedside and treat him like an invalid. By the time St Aldric had healed, there would be no parting the two of them.

It was no decision at all, really. Doctor Hastings must stay in residence, until the patient improved.

Chapter Thirteen

On her way down to breakfast, Eve paused to listen at the door of her father's study. It was unusual to have him up and working at such an hour. And even more strange that there was a visitor involving him in heated conversation. It was stranger still that the visitor would be Sam.

They were arguing. *Please, do not let it be about me.* The situation was difficult enough without dragging Father into it. She had not been able to stop thinking about Sam's words in the carriage. Perhaps she did wish to continue her education after marriage. Her curiosity would not be so easy to kill as Michael thought. He would adjust in time to her ways. At least, she hoped he would. But either way, it did not mean that she wished to run away with Sam.

It might, of course. But she wouldn't want him bothering Father about it, until she had given the matter more thought. And with St Aldric still asleep in the guest room, they dare not try to settle anything today.

She leaned close to the panel and caught snatches of conversation.

'I simply think that it would be better to find another man for the job.' Her father was reasonable, but cross.

'I imagine you would. It makes you that uncomfortable, does it, to have me back in the house?' Sam was truly angry and more sarcastic than she'd ever heard him.

'Of course not,' her father replied in a voice best described as uncomfortable.

'Well, it should. Everything you told me was a lie. If you have any conscience at all, I hope it is bothering you.'

'At the time, it seemed the easiest course.'

'Easy?' Sam was not just angry. He was irate. 'You deserve to suffer some small bit of the torment I've known for the last six years. That you would allow me to believe—'

No matter the current difficulties between them all, he had no right to speak to her father in such a way. Unable to contain herself, Eve burst through the door. 'Sam!' She was angry at herself as well, for ever wanting to return to him. He had known of his true parentage for less than a week and the man she thought she'd known had become a spiteful, ungrateful whelp to the man who'd raised him. 'Cease this arguing immediately. It can be heard in the hall.'

'What? What have you heard?' Her father went white.

She turned to Sam, who was clearly the one at fault. 'I am shocked, Dr Hastings, that you would come here, before we have even breakfasted, to make a row about things that happened years ago.'

The two men glanced at each other in silence. Then Sam said, in a more moderate tone, 'I did not come here of my own volition. I was summoned.'

'By whom?' She laughed. 'I did not call you, if that is what you have been claiming.'

Her father stood and came around the desk to

take her by the hand. 'It was the duke, Evelyn. His condition has worsened. He did not want to wake us and sent for the doctor.'

'Ill?' A hundred possibilities flashed through her mind. And the most unworthy one shouted the loudest. *If he dies, I will not have to choose.*

It was horrid of her. The choice had already been made and she was happy with it. Michael was a wonderful man. A saint. What sort of woman was she, to even consider his death?

'You needn't worry,' Sam said. 'He will recover.' His voice was soothing. It was his doctor voice, she was sure, meant to keep the family from worry.

'If there is anything I can do, any medicine I can send for, other physicians who specialise…' Her father was not calmed at all by it.

'As I told you before, Lord Thorne, I am quite capable of dealing with a case of mumps in my own brother.' So this was what had upset Sam. Her father had questioned his skill. But at least he had acknowledged that the duke was kin.

'It will be fine, Father,' Eve said. But she felt not so much calm, as numb. 'Sam is right. He can handle this easily. And Michael asked specifically for him.' That was a good sign, wasn't it? At least the two of them were not at odds.

'Very well, then,' Thorne responded, still sounding frosty. 'You are here in my house again at the request of the duke and there is nothing I can do about it. What do you prescribe, Dr Hastings?'

'Keep the curtains drawn and the staff away from him. There is no one on that floor of the house, is there?'

'We have no other guests,' said her father.

'Then send Tom to the inn for my chest and some fresh linen. I will occupy one of the empty rooms, since I have no fear of contagion. But I recommend you keep your distance, Lord Thorne, just as you did when Evelyn and I suffered through this as children. If you cannot specifically remember having this illness as a child, you must not come in contact with the infected.'

'But surely, a duke…' Her father was shaking his head in amazement, as though he believed that there was something about a peerage that should render one impervious to the ills of lesser men.

'Sam is right. You needn't worry, Father. I will stay with the pair of them, night and day, to make sure their needs are met.' Both men started at her offer, as though she was not capable of helping.

'That will hardly be necessary,' Thorne said.

'I agree with your father,' Sam said hurriedly.

'There is no risk to me, Sam,' she reminded him. 'As you just reminded Father, I had the disease as a child, same as you. And, Father, I would do the same for any other guest that fell ill under our roof.'

'But, Evie,' Sam said, using the calm voice again, 'your presence will not heal him any faster.'

'He is my betrothed,' Eve said, using the same calming tones that he was using on her. 'And he needs me.' After their last conversation, she was sure Sam did not want to hear that. But it was the truth. Even if it might change in the future, she would not argue it out in front of her father. Nor could she abandon Michael as he lay ill.

Thorne was looking at Sam now, leaving the decision to him. He was clearly against the idea, but did not want to be the one responsible for refusing her.

And Sam just looked tired. Of course, he had been up in the middle of the night to care for Michael. Perhaps it had nothing to do with her. 'She will take no harm in staying with him. And it is better than having a series of maids trailing in and out of the room, cutting up the peace. Having her at his side might steady him and alleviate some of the discomfort.'

'But it is hardly proper,' her father argued.

'Oh, please, Father. Michael is in no condition to compromise me.' It occurred to her that Sam was another matter entirely. But surely he would not trouble her in her own home with her future husband just down the hall. She put her doubts aside. 'You know I will be a help, for this is hardly different from what I accomplish when we are in the country.'

'That is with women and children,' her father said, aghast. 'St Aldric is a grown man.'

Sam cleared his throat to indicate the delicacy

of the subject. 'I will tend the more personal needs of the patient myself. There is no dishonour in tending the ill.'

'Very well, then,' Thorne said with a sigh. 'You have my permission, Evelyn.'

As if his permission had been what she was requesting. She would do it with or without their consent. But if it made him feel better to think he could control her, so be it.

'She will be of aid to me,' Sam affirmed. 'And we will limit his contact with other, more susceptible members of the household, by caring for him ourselves. We will also limit gossip, for I doubt he will wish to be seen by others in his current condition.'

'This is true,' her father said, obviously encouraged. 'It is better to keep such things in the family and away from prying eyes.'

'Then it is settled,' Evelyn said with a smile. 'I shall tell Mrs Abbott to close off the third floor until such time as Sam deems it safe. Meals may be brought to the head of the stairs and I will see to it that they are eaten. A maid can come in once a day to change the linen and that will be that.'

Now her father was nodding along with the scheme, as though he had thought of it himself. And perhaps, at the end of it, she would have proved to Michael that her use in a sick room was far more important a pastime than remaining quiet in the dining room.

Once Evie had gone to make arrangements for the sick ward, Sam had no desire to continue the conversation he'd been having with Lord Thorne. His efforts to remain calm while notifying the man of his sick guest had quickly degenerated into a shouting match. It had been all he could do to be polite before he'd learned the truth of his parentage, but now he could not stand the man. If Evie had arrived a moment later, she'd have heard him bring forth every sordid detail of his parting, for he'd meant to confront Thorne with the effects of his casual lies and make him see what they had done to his daughter's happiness. With a warning glare to let the man know their business was not finished, he left to pay another visit to his patient.

St Aldric's condition had worsened since the

previous evening. The swelling of the jaw was more pronounced as the duke stirred in his sleep in obvious discomfort. In his mind Sam ticked through the more extreme complications and prayed that he would not see them. Deafness and sterility were not uncommon. And despite what he had told the Thornes, rare cases turned fatal. Although he had no desire to be personal physician to the man, neither did he want to be the one responsible for the death of a peer.

But some things were inevitable.

He examined the thought, rejected it and examined it again. Nature would have its way, no matter what he attempted. But if he helped it along? No one would be the wiser. He had already dispensed with the witnesses who might question him, in the name of quarantine. An incorrect dosage of many of the medicines in his bag would be more weakening than strengthening. A bleeding, taken too far, was no different than a war wound. A knick in an artery would have the life of the patient drained away before the flow could be staunched.

If the duke died, Evie was no longer betrothed.

After a period of mourning, she would be free to do as she wished. Thorne could not stop them. The only reason he'd found to separate them had been revealed as a lie. If he tried to find another objection, Sam would counter it. Or he could threaten to reveal the truth. What would the man do to keep Evie from learning that the father she worshipped and adored would stoop so low?

Murder and blackmail both. He sat in the chair at the side of the bed, horrified at his own thoughts. He had thought for ages that his love for Evie was some sort of spiritual disease. But it had been innocent, compared to his current state of mind.

Perhaps he was the one who needed treatment. Or perhaps this was what true temptation felt like, when one had the means at hand to do true evil. He had but to disregard the oath he had taken to do no intentional harm and take a life.

It was beneath unworthy. He looked again at the prone figure, the swollen jaw and the shadows under eyes. The man was suffering already and would likely suffer more. It was his job to help.

And as he had argued in Thorne's office, this was not merely a peer, this man was his brother.

His blood. He stared at the sleeping face and the strange similarities to his own. Suppose it had been he lying there and St Aldric holding the poison bottle. He'd have nothing to fear. The man was a saint.

Or so it appeared. In his darkest hour, no living man was capable of the purity ascribed to St Aldric. But his ability to behave admirably, in words and actions, was the very opposite of Thorne. His pretended father had been willing to stoop to unimagined depths when provoked. If Sam was to be forced into a different family, there was comfort in knowing that it might be one where truth and honour had value.

But to accept the bond was to accept the duty. To be worthy of it, he should not meet honesty with deceit. Not today, perhaps. But when the patient was recovered, there would be a difficult but necessary discussion about the future of Lady Evelyn Thorne. 'Pax,' he whispered, laying a hand on St Aldric's forehead.

Still hot. Perhaps a cool drink should accompany the next round of laudanum.

In response, the duke stirred and opened his eyes. He winced as though the light hurt him and touched his cheek with his hand, only to pull back in pain. When on a sickbed, a peer looked like any other patient. He was frightened and alone, though he did a decent job of hiding the fact. Stripped to his nightshirt and flat on his back, he looked smaller than he had in the study. Sam did his best to ignore the fact. It was no consolation to be the taller man, if this was the only way it could be achieved.

'I hoped it had been a dream,' St Aldric said, in a scratchy voice.

'I am sorry, but, no.'

'Is there anything more that can be done?' He was not irritable. He was stoic in the face of the illness, neither blaming God nor the doctor, as some of his patients had been prone to do.

'Ice for the fever,' Sam said simply. 'A poultice for the swelling, or perhaps a good bleeding.'

The duke winced again.

'Laudanum and belladonna for the pain. You

would not want a bolus, I assure you. Your throat will be too raw to take it easily. No strong spirits without my permission. Later, I will allow a draught of negus. For the most part, this is a thing to be borne and not cured. It will pass. In a week you will be better. But you will be in bed for two.'

The duke settled back into the pillows. 'There will be no lasting effects?'

And here was the question Sam did not want to answer. It was far too soon to tell. He turned back the sheet and looked down to examine the swelling, which was not yet great, but would grow worse.

The duke gave a gasp, half-pain and half-alarm, and tried to sit up.

Sam raised the sheet and pushed him back down on the bed. 'You would do better not to look. It will only upset you and will do nothing to speed recovery. But I expect you hurt, do you not?'

'Yes.' Now the duke's voice was small and childlike, near to a whimper.

'It is part of the disease. And one that you would not have had to bear, had you taken this infection as a child. I cannot tell you how bad it might become. But I will do everything in my power to minimise the problem.'

Although there was damn little he could do, now that it had begun. He measured a few drops of opiate into a large glass of spirits and pressed it into the duke's hand. 'Here. Drink.'

The duke took a sip. 'Vile stuff to have at breakfast,' he said, making a face.

'It is good that you stayed ashore, then,' Sam said, with a grim smile. 'I would not say that I cured everything with rum while on board the *Matilda*, but it seldom made the situation any worse.'

'If that is all that there is to it, then any man might be a physician.'

'You should be glad that it is all you need. It took only one battle to prove me handy with a saw and a needle. You will escape with all your limbs intact.'

'All save one,' the duke reminded him and took another drink.

He knew, then. And had already begun to fear.

'We cannot be sure of that problem for quite some time, your Grace.'

'Do not coddle me,' the duke barked, then added more quietly, 'And do not tell Evelyn.'

It was quite possible that Evie knew already. If she did not, it would not be long before she looked it up in one of the texts she claimed to have and learned that a union with St Aldric might well be childless. 'I will say nothing, your Grace.'

The duke sighed again. 'My name is Michael.'

Sam froze for a moment, then busied himself with his instruments, pretending that he had not heard.

'I request that you use it. Under the circumstances, it seems rather ridiculous to hear the title from you. You are family, after all.'

Family.

There was that word again. Sam had spent his life alternately assuming the Thornes were his family and praying that they were not. When he had returned to London, he would have chosen anyone in the world but the man in front of him to claim as kin. His plan had been to dislike St Aldric quite thoroughly.

Yet on talking to the man, he could not have wanted a better brother. Other than proposing to Evie, *Michael* had given him no reason for hatred. 'You would not prefer to be called Saint?'

The duke tried to laugh, winced again and gave him a feeble smile. His eyes were losing their brightness. The medicine was taking effect. 'Do you think it will keep me from blasphemy to remind me of that?'

'Having dealt with men in pain, I doubt it. Michael,' he added, trying not to feel uncomfortable. 'You may curse all you like, if you think it will help.'

'And might I call you Samuel?'

Sam would rather he not. It was too personal. And too soon. But if it was the only comfort he could offer, then it was cruel to deny it. He nodded. 'Or Sam, as Lady Evelyn does.'

'The fair Lady Evelyn.' The duke settled back into his pillows with a contented smile, intending to dream of Evie as he drifted towards narcotic slumber. It was only natural for a man to think of his fiancée at such a time.

Sam knew exactly the dreams in the duke's

mind, for he'd had them himself. Each night, he had lain in his bunk, cursing himself for imagining her soft, white shoulders pressed to his chest, her lips on his skin and her sighs as she slept beside him. He needn't have bothered with self-recrimination. It had been a harmless diversion, after all.

Sam reached to take the half-empty medicine cup from the duke's sagging hand. As he did so, St Aldric opened his eyes again, pulled it back and raised it in a toast to Sam. 'And to my brother, Dr Sam Hastings, who could as easily poison me with the stuff in his bag as cure me. Arsenic. Mercury. Opium. No one would know the difference.'

His unguarded words startled Sam. But had he not told himself just the same? 'I would never… I have taken an oath, you know.'

'But I bet you wish you hadn't.' The duke toasted him again and their eyes met over the rim. Then he very deliberately drained the glass to the dregs.

That was true as well. A few moments ago, he had stood over his patient and contemplated murder. And, worse yet, the duke knew it. That had been what the curious look on his face had meant just now. It was one-part trust that a brother would not kill a brother. And one-part dare to remind him that, should it happen just such a way, the Saint would understand.

Peer or no, the man was either mad or as fearless as any of the marines on board ship. And now his eyes were truly closing, his head drooping on the pillow. Sam took the glass away and walked quietly from the room to see how Evie had got on in her preparations.

She was standing at the top of the stairs. Her father was still beside her, shifting nervously from foot to foot, afraid to abandon his daughter in a sick ward. They watched him approach. By their worried looks, his conflicting emotions were still plain on his face. They could read death there. And they feared that his moment of weakness was a reflection on the gravity of the duke's disease.

He took a moment to pull his mind out of the dark place it was lurking, and carefully masked his true feelings as he might for the family of any patient.

'How is he?' Evelyn asked.

'Sleeping again,' Sam said, back in command. If a doctor could do nothing else, he must at least appear to be in control of the situation. Especially if it was one that was likely to inflict harm or cure itself, no matter what he might do. 'But he was concerned that you would be frightened by the extent of his illness.'

Evie made a huffing noise, as though diminishing the duke's concern. 'He should not waste the energy. You will care for him and he will be fine.'

At least for the moment, she had forgotten that she was angry with Sam. She needed his help. And she was looking at him with the worshipful confidence she had held when he was her hero and she a troublesome little pest.

If he had acted on his base desires to do away with St Aldric, she would discover it. She would look once into his eyes and would know, and she would never look at him like this again. If he also shared Thorne's duplicity, that man would lose her trust as well. The punishment was deserved. But some things were too cruel to be just.

He gave her a solemn nod. 'He will be fine.'

She cast a worried glance down the hall to the sick room. 'Would it help him, if I sat with him for a time?'

Sam shrugged. 'It would not hurt. If it gives you comfort to do so, then I have no objections.' Not as a physician, at least. He was properly envious of any man who awoke to an angel at his bedside. 'If he is asleep, do not wake him. If he wakes on his own, do not allow him to become excited.'

She turned from him and hurried towards the room that held her betrothed, eager to tend him. Her father cast a worried glance after her.

'She will be fine,' he assured Thorne again. 'But you must keep your distance. If you feel any symptoms of the illness, or notice them in others, notify me immediately and segregate the effected persons to this floor of the house.'

'Is it really so serious a sickness, then?' Thorne was worried for his daughter's future and the possible end to his carefully constructed plans.

'Bad enough so that I would not wish it on an otherwise healthy man. Chances are excellent that he will recover.'

'But a full recovery...' Thorne gave him another worried look. 'I have heard of men who have had this difficulty. And they lived, of course, but there were consequences.'

Sam nodded, for he could not lie when confronted with a fact. But for now, their differences were moot compared to the reassurance he owed this man on the health of his guest. 'We will not know of problems until much later. It is why I insist on the quarantine and not upsetting the patient. He is already brooding on the possible outcome. And he should not, until he is stronger.'

Thorne nodded in agreement. 'You are right in this. Better that we let Evie keep his spirits up than to have a ring of worried faces around the bedside.'

'Very good. Now go,' Sam said, as gently as possible. 'We will send word if there is a change. But it will do him no good if you sicken as well. Trust us.' *Trust me.* 'He shall have the best possible care.'

'And about before…?' Thorne gave him another worried look.

'Now is not the time to continue that particular discussion,' Sam said, fighting the rage and disgust that still boiled beneath his professional calm.

'If you are alone with Evelyn and she should learn…' Thorne was hardening again, trying to regain control. His tone was both warning and threat. Although what he had left to threaten with, Sam was not sure.

'At the moment, the past is the last thing I wish to speak of. I have a patient, sir, and you have a guest who is ill. We must do what is best for him. There is nothing more between us than that.'

'And Evelyn?' he said again. 'Do you want what is best for her as well?'

'I fear we disagree on what that might be,' Sam said. 'For I would not lie to her, as you did to me. But neither will I dredge up the past, to win her. I will not speak on it.'

Still Thorne hovered, as though he expected Sam's betrayal before he could reach the second-floor landing.

'You have my word,' Sam added, his jaw clenching, 'as the son of the late Duke of St Aldric.' The oath was foreign to him. But he felt the weight of it as it left his lips. Family honour. How strange to have found it, after all this time. 'Now go.'

Without another word, Thorne turned and went down the stairs.

Chapter Fourteen

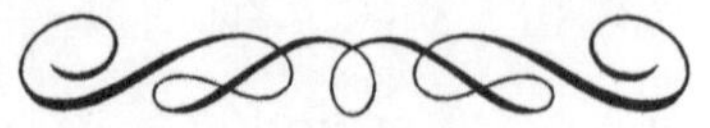

St Aldric looked terrible.

Eve could see why he had wanted to protect her from the truth. She had dealt with the disease in children, but in a grown man it looked far worse. If she had been the sort of weak woman he expected, she would have been shocked by the extent of the swelling and burst into sympathetic tears. She would have upset herself and made things more difficult for everyone involved.

Instead, she sat in the chair at the bedside and gathered his limp hand into her own.

He slept on, unaware of her presence.

Oh, Michael, what am I going to do with you? Although she had not wanted to admit it, this engagement was a mistake. She should never have yielded to Father's insistence. She should have found another way.

But it was quite possible that choosing Sam instead would be exchanging a bad mistake for a worse one. In some ways, he was just as she remembered. But the calm assurance she felt around him had faded. He was erratic: calm one moment, shouting the next, hating her father while he claimed to love her, offering no explanation as to why he had gone and why he found her suddenly irresistible once she belonged to another.

She needed time to think and it appeared that she would have at least a week trapped with the pair of them to sort her feelings.

She gave Michael's hand a squeeze, but he barely stirred. For good measure, she sponged his hot forehead with water from the basin, adjusted his covers and put her head to his chest to listen to his breathing, which was deep and regular. Sam had been right. There was nothing she could do right now.

She left the room and went out into the hall, glancing down it to the open door at the back of the house. It was a bedroom with an attached parlour that would be a logical place for the pair of them to sit while waiting for the duke to awake.

She gave an involuntary shiver at the thought. She had been eager to be alone with Sam a week ago, but now she was not sure how she felt. Still eager, apparently, for the shiver had been one of excitement. But she felt guilty as well. Poor Michael had no one but the two of them. And he was ill. It was very bad to be thinking of her own wants and needs, while he suffered.

Sam was sitting at a table by the fireplace, his medical bag at his feet, reviewing a text, and looking like the competent healer he was. Despite the strange way he acted towards her, he was a good man as well.

She did not wish to interrupt him in his work. But really, how much study would he need to handle something so common? And was such intent concentration necessary? 'Are you trying to avoid talking to me?' she asked.

He smiled into his book at being caught. 'I have been reading the same page over and over for an hour, waiting for you to return. How is the patient?'

'Still asleep.'

'Very good. I will look in on him later.' He closed the book and set it aside, then looked at her expectantly.

What did he want her to say? 'Thank you for this,' she said, in a sombre voice.

'For doing my job?' he asked.

'For doing this particular job. I am sure it must be hard for you.'

'The duke requested me,' Sam said, deliberately misunderstanding her. 'After making the initial visit, it makes no sense to turn the case over to another.'

'I mean because of me,' she said.

'On the contrary—' he was smiling again '—I am quite at ease in your presence, Lady Evelyn. I think it is you who are uncomfortable.'

It was true, of course. But he was being deliberately provoking in pointing it out. 'I will manage,' she said, not allowing herself to be baited. 'And you can leave off calling me Lady Evelyn. Things are difficult enough without that.'

His lips twitched. 'Very well, Evie.'

'It is good that we are all here together.' She gave a firm nod. 'It will give you a chance to know your brother better.' And show some sign of love for him, so that she did not feel quite so foolish at insisting they know the truth. 'I am sure, once you have spent time with him…'

'That the same problem will exist between us,' Sam finished. 'He is engaged to the woman I love.'

'You are most free with that word of late,' she said.

'Better late than never.'

He was treating this newfound love as if it were a joke. 'But still, it is quite different from the six years of silence and the lust you claimed on your return.'

'Anything I said, was said because I wanted what was best for you,' he replied.

'And you have changed, now that I am engaged to another?'

'I have changed because I recently discovered that what was best for you was to be married to me.' He sounded very calm and very sure of himself, but it was really no answer at all.

'If you mean because of the business at dinner the other night, I do not believe you. You started speaking words of love a full day before that.'

He shook his head. 'I came to the conclusion before then. Dinner simply confirmed it.'

'Are you implying that Michael did something to render himself less than a suitable match for me?'

Sam laughed. 'No. The brother you found for me continues to be perfect. He is just not perfect for you.'

'And you are?' She had thought so herself, until very recently.

'No man is perfect,' he said. 'But I would try to be, for your sake.'

'That is not very different from the promises that Michael made when he was courting me,' Eve said. But his words had never made her heart flutter, as Sam's did.

'And how is that working so far?' Sam asked innocently. 'Since he is already deemed a saint, it does not seem likely he will have to alter much.

But you, Evie?' He smiled again. 'You are most delightfully flawed. And I would not change a bit of you.'

It was just as she had thought, on the day he arrived. He was more honest than flattering. But there was so much love for her behind his words that she would rather hear criticisms from him than compliments from another.

'And while we are on the subject of your deficiencies,' he said with a smile, 'there was one I should have corrected when we spoke in the garden. You are quite wrong about our first kiss.'

'I was not.' If she was sure of nothing else, it was the moment that changed her life.

'Our first kiss was about a week before the time you remember. You were standing in the library, by the big windows, trying to reach a book on the top shelf without using the ladder. I came upon you suddenly, with the sunlight outlining your body, and for a moment I did not know you at all. I saw nothing but a beautiful young woman: an angel in a nimbus of light.'

'I do not remember any of this,' she said, shaking her head.

He gave a small snort. 'Of course you would not. You cared for nothing but getting the book.' Then he sighed, lost in a pleasant memory. 'But my eyes were opened to the promise of manhood. Then you turned your head and were my little Evie again, demanding that I help you.'

'And did you?' she asked, honestly curious.

He gave a small bow. 'Ever your servant, Lady Evelyn. I got you the book. You rewarded me with a kiss on the lips. Then you ran off as if nothing had happened. You might as well have ripped the heart out of my chest and taken it as well. I have not been the master of it, from that moment.'

'But the time in the garden?' For she was sure that she remembered it quite clearly.

'Was the first time I kissed you,' he answered. 'I planned for a full week, trying to find a way to ask if you might ever feel for me what I had come to feel for you. But my words failed me, each time. So I let my actions speak. And I had my answer.'

The kiss had made her feel just as she was feeling now. It was as if she was seeing Sam truly for the first time. He loved her. She loved him. And it had been so for ages. Why had she not seen it before?

She had. It was he who had been denying it. 'You said you did not remember.'

'I lied.'

'How very convenient,' she said, still not sure.

'I've told you many lies, since I returned.' But he did not seem the least bit ashamed by his admissions. 'Here, I will prove it to you. Would you like me to recite for you? I know the contents of your letters as well as any poem.'

He had heard her, as she poured out her heart to him for six lonely years. He had not answered, but at least he had listened. 'You read them?'

'Every word.' He smiled. 'They gave such comfort. You have no idea. When one went astray, or arrived out of order, I sat in a fog of despair, until the next came to cheer me again. You begged me over and over to answer. You grew angry with my silence and, at least once a year, you told me I was horrible and swore that I would hear no more from you.'

His smile disappeared. 'I dreaded those letters.

Suppose, this time, you were sincere? Suppose my negligence had finally cost me my Evie?' He relaxed. 'But in a week, or perhaps two, you wrote again.' And tensed at another bad memory. 'In November of 'sixteen you were silent the whole month. But December brought another letter and a muffler so hideous I must assume you were the one who made it.'

Unable to stop herself, she gave a small joyful laugh, for he was finally saying what she had longed to hear. 'You have come back to me, after all?'

'I never left,' he whispered. 'I tried, but I could not.'

She had meant only to talk. To consider rationally, take her time and make the best decisions possible. Then she would have to break with one man or the other. But she would do it so gently that they might all be friends.

Instead, she seized Sam Hastings by the shirt front and kissed him.

It took no further encouragement for him to kiss her back. These were the kisses she had been waiting a lifetime for. More passionate than the sweet kiss of youth and more tender than the eager grappling of the last few days. Quick pecks on her face and throat, and slow forays into her mouth. His tongue thrust. It circled. It remained perfectly still, resting against her lips. And through it all he smiled. His breath came in deep, satisfied sighs and silent laughs of relief.

His arms were about her, neither too tight nor too loose. But she clung to his, afraid that he would escape. Sam was home. Not the strange imposter that had walked in the door. This was *her* Sam. And she would never let him get away.

He was pulling her back towards the door to the bedroom. And each step was like waltzing, if that dance could be done with bodies held so indecently close. She rubbed herself against him, pressing her breasts to his chest. He kissed her shoulder and cupped her bottom so that their hips bumped together.

For a moment, they both paused in shock. The brief contact was too good not to repeat. He brought their hips together again and they pressed into each other. Her knees buckled at the thought of them, joined.

He supported her, still holding her tight as he backed into the bedroom and shut the door. Then he shrugged out of his coat, stepping on it, and over, as it fell to the floor. She kicked out of her slippers, leaving them behind as well. And suddenly they were a frenzy of hands undoing buttons, untucking shirts and dropping garments as they came free of them. By the time they reached the bed, she was in shift and stockings, and he was shirtless and kicking free of his boots.

He had a manly chest. She had known he must look somewhat like the paintings she had seen of naked men. But pictures did not teach her the feel, or the taste, or the way he would laugh as she ran her fingers over his ribs and he caught at her hands to kiss them.

Then he rolled, pulling her with him, pushing her down on her back as his hands went to his buttons. He kissed her mouth again, pulling down his breeches and lying naked on top of her, heavy and hard between her legs.

The curtains were drawn and the room was gloomy, but hardly dark. If she wished, she could see him and watch as he loved her. Why was she closing her eyes when there was so much to learn? She opened them wide, so that she would not miss a thing.

He seemed to sense this, pulling away and laughing again, flicking her nose with his finger before kneeling above her as he untied her garters and rolled her stockings down her legs.

'You are not like the illustrations in the medical books,' she said, amazed.

'I am like them in all the ways that matter,' he said, in a voice that was deliberately lecherous. 'You are not like the books, either. You are the most beautiful woman I have ever seen.' He pulled her shift over her head. 'But that is exactly as I imagined you'd be. Do not be afraid,' he whispered.

She laughed at him. For when had she ever been frightened of Sam?

He growled and lay on top of her again, sliding down, holding a breast in each hand and taking the nipples into his mouth. If he meant to punish her for laughing, he was doing it wrong. This was only making her more excited, even when he bit her. She would not mind if they stayed like this for ever.

He stopped. He kissed her navel. And then he hooked his arms around her legs, spread them and kissed.

This was different. It tickled. But it was a new sort of ticklishness that seemed to travel over her whole body. She giggled. Then she laughed. She forced her fist into her mouth, trying to keep back the screaming, gasping, silent gales of laughter. She hooked one leg over his shoulder, trying to hold him still, and pounded her fists into the mattress and panted, trying to get control of herself. His kisses were unrelenting. If he did not stop, she was not sure what would happen.

And then, it did. Suddenly, everything changed. She could breathe again, but she did not want to. She just wanted to lie perfectly still and feel like this for ever.

He did not seem the least bit surprised at what had happened. He pulled away from her and grabbed a pillow from the bed, lifting her hips and sliding it under her. Then he bent her knees so that her feet were close to her body. 'This will make it easier,' he said.

She could not manage to say anything at all. His fingers were where his mouth had been, spreading the wetness and slipping inside, stretching her.

She did not want his fingers, she wanted more. She held out her arms and reached down until her fingers brushed his manhood. She steeled her nerve and explored, running a finger down the length and cupping his testicles.

His fingers froze, then pushed deeper as he leaned forwards, muttering, 'Damn! I meant to teach you to love me. Did you learn that from an anatomy book? Never mind. I do not care. Oh God, woman, do not stop.'

She ran her hands over him again. 'I want this.'

'A moment more.' He sighed, letting her caress him. Then he withdrew his fingers and took her hands, placing them between her legs and encouraging her to touch herself. It felt good.

The next moment, he was hovering over her and there was a slow push. She tightened her body, and could feel him inside of it. They were finally together. Her body twitched under her fingers, and tightened again, as he moved.

His body began to shake. There were a few hurried thrusts and he shuddered a second time, swearing, trembling and collapsing in her arms as she felt the rush of his seed inside her.

He lay still for a time, holding her, as weak and spent as she was. Then he rolled without leaving her body, pulling her with him so she was half-sprawled on top of him. He fumbled a blanket up to cover them. Then he kissed her shoulder. 'The next time will be different.'

She pushed against him. 'I should hope not. I liked this.'

He was laughing now, so hard that his body was trembling again. 'Show some decorum, Lady Evelyn. You are far too eager for a girl who was a virgin only a few moments ago.'

'Well, I was,' she said, with a frown. 'And it is most rude of you to imply otherwise.'

'Darling, I know,' he said, still laughing.

'How…?'

'I am a doctor. I would not be much of one if I could not tell that.'

'I am sorry if I did not respond according to your assumptions,' she said a little tartly.

'You exceeded expectations,' he assured her.

'As did you,' she said, trying to sound more knowledgeable than she was.

'Then you did not expect much of me,' he said, still laughing. 'That was over before it was begun. In the future, I shall try harder to please you.'

The future. They would have a future and it would be full of this. How wonderful that would be.

'Of course, today, we did not have long. When we do this again, I will take my time.'

He stood, leaving her on the bed, and fumbled his way back into his clothes.

She held out a hand to draw him back. 'Where are you going?'

'I must check on my patient. He is most likely still asleep, for the dose I gave him was strong. But still, one must never assume.'

She sat straight up in the bed and felt the blanket fall away from her. She gathered it hastily around her. It was ludicrous to be embarrassed now, after what they had done. But she was.

She had forgotten Michael.

But, clearly, her lover had not.

Chapter Fifteen

Once Sam had gone, she gathered up her clothing, washed and dressed herself. Then she sat down on the edge of the bed and waited.

Sam returned to the room shortly, and dropped his bag on the floor near the door. 'The swelling increases, but that is to be expected. I gave him one more dose of laudanum, so that he will sleep through the worst of it. Later this afternoon, he will wake and we will treat more aggressively.'

He stopped in the doorway, finally noticing her expression.

'You are thinking of the engagement, aren't you?'

Of course she was. And it was too late to be doing so. Her personal sense of honour should have reminded her of it an hour ago. 'I betrayed Michael.'

'You have not married as yet.' Sam was so matter of fact about it. It was as if he was describing some easily cured disease.

'But I promised.'

'Then break it.' Sam sat down beside her and put an arm about her shoulder. 'You must tell him that you have made a mistake. Or would you prefer that I did? I did mean to speak to him on the subject, when he was better.' His face clouded for a moment. 'But then I had not expected things to move so quickly. Perhaps, when he wakes, I should—'

'No,' she interrupted. 'It must be me.' She was so tired of being presented with a *fait accompli*. She would not be rushed into the decision to part from Michael, as she had with the one to accept him. 'But it will not be today. He must be fully awake and healthy enough to understand.'

'Very well,' Sam said cautiously. Then he stroked her shoulders. 'But let it be soon, Evie. I love you. And I know that you love me. Now that you have felt how it can be between us, do not deny those feelings.'

'There will be a scandal,' she said. Worse than that, her father would be heartbroken.

'But we do not have to stay in London to see it. Run away with me.' The arm about her shoulder pulled her closer so he could whisper in her ear. 'Anywhere you wish to go. Scotland? Italy? The Americas? Name the place and I will take you there.'

'Would you marry me, then?' For now that they had done the deed, he did not speak of a wedding.

'Of course,' he scoffed as though he expected her to know. But how could she?

'I must say, your story has changed, since the night you told me to accept St Aldric. You swore then that you would never marry me.' She stared straight ahead, afraid of what his face might reveal.

His hand stilled on hers, and then dropped away. 'Many things have changed since that night.'

She did not want change. She wanted the constant love that she had shown to him. 'And how do I know that they will not change again, once I have broken with the duke?'

'Because I have always been yours,' he said. 'From the first, I have loved you.'

'Then why did you call it lust? And why did you refuse me, when I was free to offer you my heart?' She turned to stare at him now and waited for some clue that would reveal the truth.

His face darkened. 'At the time, I thought it was for the best. For both of us.'

'You thought for me, did you? And was I not to be consulted in my own future?' It seemed, just as her father had with St Aldric, that Sam did not think her capable of making reasoned decisions. But if she was married to the duke, he would treat her the same way.

'The situation was…' He seemed at a loss for words. 'The problem was delicate. You were promised to another man when I arrived. I did not want to interfere.'

'It is not interference if help is requested,' she said, exasperated. 'If I was promised, it was by someone else. I had nothing to do with the decision. You must have known how conflicted I was.

I all but threw myself at your feet and begged you to love me.'

'Well…yes.' This seemed to make him more uncomfortable than ardent.

'I waited for years, between heaven and hell, knowing you would come back for me and fearing you would not. Can you not offer me any explanation, other than that you thought it was for the best?' Despite what had just happened, an act which should have answered all her questions, she was still angry at him. He had distracted her with sweet words and seduced her into breaking her promise. But it had changed nothing. He had left her without explanation.

She had smothered the anger she felt, wrapping it in prayers for his safety and fantasies that he would return for her. But she remembered the letters as well as he, for she had written them. She had begged him for explanations. She had called him out on his cruelty. And, for six years, he had said nothing.

He pulled her close again, his arms about her shoulders and his lips on her throat, teasing the nerves until she shuddered. 'I suffered as well,' he whispered. 'There was no heaven for me. Only the hell of being without you. But now, everything has changed.'

She fought free of him and slid down the mattress to put distance between their bodies. 'How has it changed? What is so very different today from a few days ago?' But she feared she knew.

'I…I…I…'

Sam, who was never at a loss for words when he was refusing her, could not manage to speak.

'Is it because I am engaged to your brother?'

'He is not my brother,' Sam snapped.

'You of all people should not deny the biology of this. You share a father.'

'But we are nothing alike.' Yet he sounded confused, as though he did not know who he was any more.

'That is a shame,' she said. 'St Aldric is a wonderful man.'

'And thank you for reminding me of that now.' He was petty and sarcastic again, and not the patient loving man he had been before he'd bedded her.

'Why does Michael's presence in my life suddenly bother you?' For it was past the point where that was easy to change. 'You approved of him when you met him.'

'I had no reason not to. He has no flaws, damn the man.'

'Jealousy is unworthy of you,' Eve reminded him.

'But it is well deserved,' Sam said. 'What chance do I have to be his equal?'

'You do not need to be. You are fine, just as you are.' Was that all this had been about?

'Oh, really?' he said, with a cynical smile. 'Because you cannot seem to stop talking about him. And obviously there must be something wrong with me, because, I find, after all this time, that my father did not wish to acknowledge my existence.'

'But you must have known…' For how else did one end up in a foundling home?

'I am a nameless nobody. And he is a duke. What could I ever do to compete? What do I have that he does not?'

'Other than my maidenhead?' she asked, her

stomach feeling sick and strange. 'You have that now. And my husband never shall.'

He realised what he had said and his face seemed to crumple. 'That is not what I meant. Not at all.'

'But it is true, is it not?' It seemed quite obvious, now that she thought of it. The moment he had learned the truth about himself, everything had changed.

'Evie, it is not as you think. I have longed to lie with you, of course. Dreamed of it, my whole life.'

'In lust,' she reminded him. For had he not admitted it before?

'Love,' he insisted, now that it was too late. 'I have always loved you. When it comes to you I am unchangeable,' he said. 'I thought I was not worthy. And I tried, all my life to avoid this moment. And I failed.'

It had been the most wonderful thing to have ever happened to her and yet he had fought against it. But once they were in bed, he had known just what to do to render her senseless with desire. So senseless that she had forgotten her duty to Michael. Those lessons had not been in the medical books. 'In this time you were fighting your love for me, were you innocent as well?'

'What?' The question seemed to confuse him.

'Like a monk,' she supplied. 'Celibate. Waiting in chastity for that time we might be together.'

'Of course not.' She saw his lips twitch. He had almost laughed at her question. 'That is quite a different thing.'

'Because you are a man.'

'And because I thought that I could never have you.'

For him it must have been an easy decision. He could not have her, but he must have someone. Now that the thought was in her head, she could not help but imagine him with others, doing what they had done. And, worse yet, he had done it even as he claimed to have loved only her the whole of his life.

'So you consoled yourself with others, until the very hour that I gave up waiting. At your suggestion… No. At your demand, I publicly accepted another man,' she reminded him. 'And then, suddenly, you rediscovered your love and seduced me.'

'Evie. Evie, no.' He was shaking his head, as though he could not believe the words she was saying. 'That is not how it happened at all.'

'Then tell me, Sam. Why now?' If he had a better reason, he must tell her.

But he offered no defence.

'If you have nothing to say for yourself, then I must assume I have guessed the truth.'

He shook his head again, as though trying to turn from something unpleasant. 'I cannot tell you. I simply cannot. You must trust me when I say that it was a horrible misunderstanding on my part.'

'I must trust you?' She stood and backed away from the bed. Even now, after all she had learned, she was not sure that she could resist him if he kissed her again. 'I trusted you before, when you said that it was never to be. And look where that has got me. I am dishonouring myself and betraying a man who needs me, who wants me and who, as you have pointed out, has never given me a reason to do this. Worse yet, he is ill. Conveniently unconscious because of the drugs you are giving him, so that we would not be interrupted. I am the one who has made the mistake, Sam.'

'Evie.' He spoke it as if he thought a name from childhood was a dispensation. 'At least do not doubt my treatment. Look in your books. You will see I mean him no harm.'

'Enough.' Perhaps he was right about that one thing. But it proved only that he could answer an insult to his profession more easily than his assault on her honour. 'I am sorry. But I do not think it is for leaving you, Sam. It is for listening to you in the first place.' And with that, she went back down the hall to sit at the side of her unconscious fiancé.

Chapter Sixteen

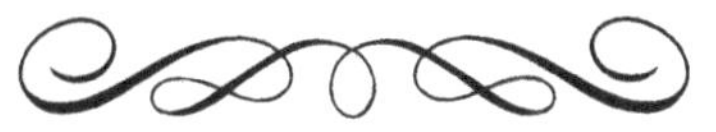

When Sam next returned to the patient's room, it was mid-afternoon. The duke was waking. And his nurse had not left his side since leaving Sam's. She'd held his hand, mopped his fevered brow. When Sam had listened at the open door, she was talking to the sleeping man in the low tones of a lover.

Now that St Aldric was conscious, she supported his head and gave him sips of iced water, tempted him with bites of custard and tried in all ways short of full confession to make up for laying with another man.

In response, St Aldric was looking up at her with the devotion of a hound, albeit a hound that had stuck his face in a beehive.

The swelling was still bad. But there was a

brightness in the duke's eyes that came from returning strength instead of fever. The worst was not over, but it was clear he would fight off the illness.

Sam had been pacing the hall for hours, trying to come up with some explanation that might mollify his lover and explain his sudden change of heart. She thought him a jealous swine who had seduced her to spoil the happiness of his brother. He was not sure, from minute to minute, how he felt about her darling Michael. But Sam was certain that man's eventual happiness had nothing to do with what had happened in the bed down the hall.

He could offer nothing, other than the truth. *Your father is a liar. He never cared for me as I thought. He was old St Aldric's toady, and he is willing to put your happiness aside to gain the favour of the Saint.*

Her father had but to deny it, as any sane man would. Then Sam would blurt the truth of what had happened and fall even lower in her estimation. She would see him either as a man low enough to lust after his own sister, or one who would make up a despicable lie, slandering her father to mask his own indifference.

He had sworn to Thorne that he would not speak. And he had done it on his true father's name. As if he could borrow that family's honour when it was convenient, and put it aside when it proved troublesome. Perhaps he was as fickle as she thought. That morning, he had been ready to make peace with St Aldric and, an hour later, he had cuckolded him while he slept. There was nothing to say that would explain any of it. He could hardly understand it himself.

He went into the sick room and stood by the bed. 'And how are you feeling after your rest, your Grace?'

From the opposite side, Evie stared at him, as protective as a lioness with a cub. 'He is doing much better, now that I am here to help,' she said, all but accusing him of doping the man insensible for his own nefarious purposes.

'I am sure he is.' It was what he'd have told any worried housewife, on visiting her husband's sick bed. Women did not like to be told that all illnesses could not be cured with love and herbs.

'It seems I have a ministering angel,' St Aldric croaked, managing a smile.

'You are most fortunate,' Sam agreed. 'But you must forgive me if I send her from the room so that I might examine you.'

'Can I not stay?' She asked it sweetly enough, but then she turned her face from St Aldric and looked daggers at him, as though she expected Sam to do away with his rival the moment she had cleared the door.

'Do not worry, my love. I am confident that my brother the physician will settle me in no time. And then, perhaps, you might come back and read to me.' The duke gave her a pale imitation of the smile he had worn at their engagement ball.

'Of course, darling.' She left reluctantly, pausing in the doorway to give him one last lingering glance, as though a quarter-hour examination would be an eternity. It was like trying to part turtle doves.

The little hypocrite.

As soon as the door was closed, Sam turned back to the patient, as eager to get this over with as they were to be rid of him. 'May I have permission to examine you, your Grace?'

The duke cocked his swollen head to the side, considering. 'Perhaps the drugs have clouded my mind, but I distinctly remember asking you to dispense with the formality of my title. There is no one to hear you, you know. You could call me anything you liked. You could even argue with me, should you have a reason to.'

Despite himself, the corners of Sam's mouth twitched in amusement. 'Do not tempt me, your Grace.'

Another sigh from the man on the bed. 'Very well, then. But please stop asking for my permission before you touch me. You know you have it. Just make me well.'

'I will do my best.' He lifted the sheet. Judging by the extent of the inflammation, it was likely that the duke would never be himself again. He carefully replaced the sheet and reached for his stethoscope.

'Doing your best,' the duke said grimly. 'That is no answer at all, is it?'

The patient's chest and heart were clear. And

his ears seemed undamaged as well. The situation was far from hopeless, although he doubted the duke would see it that way. 'Do you wish me to lie?'

St Aldric managed a false smile. 'Perhaps I do, if it means that there is a way to prevent the discussion we must have.'

Sam smiled grudgingly as well. 'I doubt it will give you comfort. I am not a very good liar, you see. I find that I get in no end of trouble trying to conceal the truth.'

'With Evelyn?'

Sam started so much that he dropped his stethoscope.

'You are right,' the duke confirmed. 'You are not a very good liar at all.'

Damn him. And damn his understanding nature. Did he not see that the whole situation was more complicated than that? And, once again, Sam had a strange desire to have a brother much like this one: older and hopefully wiser. Someone in whom he might confide the truth.

Then he remembered that he was the physician and not the patient. He was supposed to be the font of wisdom and comfort, not the receiver of it. 'I have no idea what you are talking about.'

'Of course you don't,' replied the duke in an even tone. 'But I have got you sufficiently off guard that I might get the truth out of you on my condition. We will discuss one thing or the other. What is my prognosis, doctor?'

'You should make a nearly full recovery,' Sam said, still not wanting to be pinned to an untruth.

'Nearly,' St Aldric answered flatly. 'And what part of me is not to return from this? Do me the courtesy of saying it, please.'

'There is no guarantee, one way or the other,' Sam prefaced, still not sure he wanted to commit. 'But in some cases such as yours, there is a loss of potency, or a chance of sterility.'

'I see.' There was a sort of dangerous quiet in the room and St Aldric's easy manner disappeared.

For a moment, Sam feared what any man would fear upon delivering bad news to a powerful man. There was a tendency in these things to kill the messenger. Not literally, of course. But a rumor of misdiagnosis, or malpractice, from a man of this stature would be enough to ruin him.

But the storm, if there was to be one, did not break. The tension grew and Sam added, 'There is no guarantee.'

'That will be all, for now, Doctor.' The duke glanced towards the door.

'It will be weeks, perhaps months, or longer, before you know the truth. You need to regain your strength first.'

'Before I attempt congress with Evelyn?'

Sam brought his hand down hard on the bedside table, unable to control his sudden and violent reaction to the thought.

'I know you would delay that indefinitely, if you could. Why you waste as much time as you do trying to heal me, I do not understand.'

'You asked me to,' Sam said.

The duke gave an empty laugh. 'And they call me a Saint. Perhaps nobility runs in our family.'

'Our family has nothing to do with this,' Sam said stubbornly. 'I helped you because you needed it. And now I am telling you what I would tell any man in your condition. Do not give up hope without a reason. It may take some time before we know if you are yourself again.'

'And how will I know?' Michael asked.

'If you father a child,' Sam said, cursing his own inability to offer more. 'There are no tests beyond this.'

'And if I cannot father a child?'

'Then it might be the fault of illness. Or it might have been the truth before. Or it might be the fault of the woman you are with.' Sam resisted the urge to shrug, for that was hardly a gesture that inspired confidence. 'You might have a son by the New Year. Or not.'

'You are useless,' the duke said. 'Worse than useless. Get out.'

And now he would call for another doctor. Someone who would lie to him, or bring some odd tincture that offered hope. 'You want me gone because I will not tell you what you wish to hear? You asked for the truth. It is not my fault if you do not like it.'

'Get out.'

'No.' He was refusing a direct order from a peer. It was likely professional suicide. It was illogical as well. If he cared at all for a future with the woman he loved, it made no sense to encourage this man to bed her.

But damnation, the man was his brother.

And his brother was a duke. St Aldric's glare was icy, and superior, a reminded of the difference in their ranks. 'How dare you refuse me?'

Sam sat in the chair at the bedside that Evelyn had occupied. 'I dare because I am more than a doctor to you. You wanted family, did you? Well, I have little experience with it. But from what I hear, family does not abandon family at moments like this.'

'What can you do?'

'I can say that I am sorry.'

'And what does that help?'

'You did not let me finish. I could say I was sorry that my brother is such a great blockhead. You are worrying about a future that is not certain.'

St Aldric's eyes were wide and near to panic. 'But if it is the future, do you understand what it means?'

'That all flesh is grass? That the plans of men

are not equal to the machinations of God or fate or random chance?' Sam glared down at the man in the bed. 'I have given worse news to better men than you. I have watched children die. And here you are, grieving for ones that are not even conceived. I suggest, Michael, that you accept the fact that there are things that a title will not protect you from. If you are only a saint when your faith is not tested, then you are no saint at all.'

The duke was shaking his head as though he could refuse the future he might face and have another. 'I never asked to be a saint.'

'But you have been doing a fine job up 'til now,' Sam replied. 'The only prescription I can offer you is this. You must not worry, Michael.' He put a steadying hand on the other man's shoulder. 'We will deal with other matters if they arise.'

The patient seemed somewhat mollified by his confidence that all problems could be solved with time. But that was because he could not see the confusion in Sam's heart. He had said *we*, as if he meant to be there. And before that, he had called the duke by his given name. Was there some brotherly feeling, after all? Or perhaps Evelyn was not the only one who felt guilt.

Chapter Seventeen

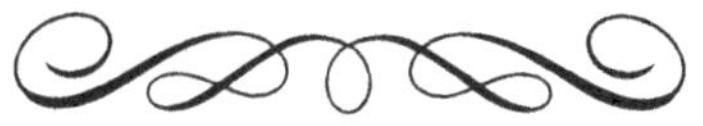

'The duke will be fine. I will be fine. Everything will be fine.'

What a weak word that was and how unlikely to be true. When she had left Michael's room her father had been lurking at the head of the stairs, eager for any news she could give him.

She had told him what he wished to hear. The duke was healing nicely and in excellent spirits. He would soon make a full recovery. She had never felt closer to him.

She had not the heart to tell Father the truth. She was not even sure she knew what the truth was herself. Sam had been evasive, when it came to the final outcome of Michael's illness. Michael was distracted, smiling to put her at ease, but clearly worried. And she was torn between the two of them: wanting one, and promised to another.

Now she was feeling the strain of unending cheerfulness in the face of problems and bemoaning, once again, the weakness of the men around her that they needed women to be happy when there was no reason to be. It must give them comfort to know that, in any situation, their wives and daughters acted like dolls with cheerful faces and lips painted shut.

If she married Michael, she had best get used to it. It was what he wished from her. He needed a wife who would smile and nod, and be as amiable as he was. She had managed several hours of it, just now, as she had tended to him. Keeping his spirits up was much more tiring than actually treating him would have been.

For the most part, she had talked nonsense. She had described the weather to him, told him about a bonnet that she meant to purchase on her next outing to Bond Street and kept him well informed on the exploits of Diana the kitten, who had caught her first mouse and been unsure what to do with it.

He had closed his eyes and smiled through most of it, informing her in a hoarse voice that it made him feel better just hearing the sound of her voice. But there was a furrow in his brow that made her suspect he would as soon have been alone and in silence.

How would he have felt if she'd given him any inkling of what had happened between her and Sam only hours before? He was dispirited enough without her begging forgiveness for her betrayal and informing him of the need to break the engagement immediately.

And now Sam was alone in the room with him. Although she had asked him not to, it was possible that he was telling the duke everything, settling the matter of her future between them. If not that, then what did he have to do that she could not witness?

She returned to the sitting room and glanced at the medical book Sam had been reading. If he was not in any way worried about the outcome, then what need did he have to study? She had heard that it was more serious for adults. But how, exactly? Michael had looked miserable, but no worse than she had been when she'd had this. She sat down on the couch and took up the book from the cushion where it rested, opening it to the marked page and reading what he had read.

'Evie!' It was Sam again, back from his examination. And he was using the warning tone that hinted she was meddling in things she did not understand. But the information was quite clear, as were the likely repercussions.

She closed the book closed with a snap of the cover and stared at him, searching for any signs that he was treating this patient differently than any other. 'You have been underestimating the severity of the disease, Sam. Or have you merely understated it?'

'It does no good to alarm the patient overly on a thing that cannot be predicted or changed.' His expression was grave, but there was nothing in it that indicated another reason to avoid the truth.

'But you must understand how serious the matter is.'

'Of course,' he replied. 'A man's potency is always of great import.'

'I mean to Michael, specifically.'

'Because you were to marry him?'

After what had happened, it was right to speak of that in the past tense. But with this fresh piece of news, her conscience strained in a different direction. 'It is of concern to me, of course,' she said, cautiously. 'But for St Aldric? You might not see…'

'Because I am only a bastard,' Sam added.

'Do not speak so,' Evie snapped. 'It is unworthy of you. The man is your brother.'

'Half-brother,' Sam reminded her. It was a matter-of-fact correction. The anger that had been present in his voice before was gone.

'Then you should have, at least, half a filial sympathy for him,' she said. 'Michael has spoken to me frequently on the subject of his family. Or, more importantly, his lack of family. He is quite conscious of the fact that there are no other members of it, save for you. It is why, when I realised the truth, I insisted that Father tell you immediately.'

'For him,' Sam said, as though this were some damning bit of evidence and not common sense.

'And for you. You deserved to know as well.'

Even if he was being an infant in worrying about the particulars, it had been cruel of Father to raise him in ignorance. 'Right now, I am explaining why it was important for *Michael*. And why he is so eager to know you better. He is very alone.'

'We are all alone,' Sam said, as though it did not matter.

'But if we need not be?' she said, hoping that a little encouragement might make him understand. 'Discovering he has a half-brother eased his mind. But it will not help him in his most important job. He needs, above all else, to produce an heir.'

'For him, or for you?' Sam asked, the jealousy she had longed to see two weeks ago in full flower. 'Because if you wish children, I would be happy to provide you with them.' He was looking at her hungrily now and she could not decide whether to be excited or appalled.

'He needs a son for the sake of the people he is responsible to,' she said, shaking her head in disgust. 'Think of something other than yourself for a moment. He has tenants, servants and a seat in

Parliament. Who will take on the responsibility of these, if he has no son to follow him?'

'Such a problem is years in the future,' Sam said dismissively.

'But to him, it is no more than a day. He thinks of the future as a matter of course.'

'The great man is so far above us that he does not live minute to minute?' Sam gave her an incredulous smile.

'In short, yes. You cannot think that I did not give this thought as well, when I agreed to marry him.' Because she was to have been a duchess. She hoped that it did not sound like she longed for the power attached to the role, but it would be a lie to say that she had not contemplated the advantages as well as the disadvantages.

'All the more reason to handle this situation with delicacy, your Grace.' It seemed with each effort to explain he became more insecure and not less. 'Just now, I discussed the possible outcome with him. I sent you from the room, so as not to embarrass him. He would not want you to see him as less than a man.'

It was another cause for exasperation. Men

acted as though their only value lay between their legs. She would never understand them. 'But he knows,' she said, dragging Sam back to the facts.

'Did you think I meant to withhold the information permanently?' He laughed. 'It is not as if I would tell him an untruth, in an effort to manipulate this situation.' His smile faded. 'That was exactly what you thought. And it was why you read the book. You did not trust me to do the right thing.'

'You have lied to me before,' she said. 'Why should I trust you to tell the truth to him?' And how could she trust him with their secret?

He sat down on the chair opposite, a blank expression on his face. 'The duke's illness, and the way I choose to treat him, has nothing to do with us. When I came home, I loved you, Evie. I had never stopped loving you. I wanted to tell you how I felt. But the time was not right for that. I had to lie. You would not have understood the truth.'

'And now things have changed,' she said. 'Tell me everything.'

He wavered for a moment. Then he said, 'You

must trust me—whatever I did, I did with your happiness in mind. I mean to be truthful from now on. And I have not lied to St Aldric about the consequences of his illness.'

'But you said you would not discuss the future with St Aldric, if it impedes his recovery?'

'You are talking about our future, I suppose,' Sam said, a grim smile on his face.

'Things must remain as they are until he is on the road to recovery. Then, perhaps we will try to discuss what recent events mean to his future and to mine.'

'Perhaps?' His eyes widened. 'You don't mean to tell him what has happened between us?'

'Of course not,' she said, shocked that he would even suggest it. 'Not now, not ever. I will not tell him that I have already been unfaithful. It would crush him.'

'I seriously doubt that,' Sam said.

'If it was discovered, it would be the death of my reputation. No one can know of this, Sam. No one at all.'

'So you can have secrets, but I cannot?' He leaned back in his chair and folded his arms across his chest. 'Very well, then. Henceforth, I shall lie about nothing that you don't want me to lie about. But once we are married, this will no longer matter.'

Had he spoken of marriage today? He seemed to think that it was a foregone conclusion.

'We are getting married, Evie,' he said, filling the silence.

It should make her happy, for it was what she had always longed to hear. And making love with him had been wonderful. That, too, was everything she'd dreamed it would be. Then why could she not say yes with her whole heart? And why could he not explain his mutability?

Then she thought of Michael, who would be even more alone than ever when she left him.

'Evie?' Sam was looking at her, as if expecting that a little prodding on his part would gain him the answer he wanted to hear. He got up from his chair and joined her on the sofa. He pulled the medical book from her hands, for she had been hugging it tight as though it were a protective shield. He set it on the table and eased closer.

If he touched her, he would kiss her. And if he kissed her…

She stood up and paced to the centre of the room. 'I think, for the time being, that we had best not discuss the future, either. And as to what happened, earlier in the day?' She gave a little shake of her head, not wanting to call it for what it was. 'I think it is unwise to continue in such a manner, when things are still so unsettled.'

'We are unsettled again, are we?' He was unsmiling. 'Very well, then, Lady Evelyn. We will wait until St Aldric is recovering. But he is of a particularly strong constitution despite this illness. It will not be long. A day, perhaps. Maybe two. And then you must make a decision.'

Chapter Eighteen

'I brought you breakfast.' She smiled in at Michael, who was sitting up in bed, still dazed from sleep. When he understood that it was she, he arranged his bedclothes as modestly as an old maid. Then he gestured that she come nearer.

The poor man. The response in her mind was involuntary and she hurried to quell it. The last thing he would want at this point was her pity. Especially if, as she suspected, he was gathering strength to minimise his discomfort, so as not to alarm her. His cheeks and neck were still grossly swollen, although somewhat better than they had been.

Sam was right, it would not be long and he would be well again. 'How are you feeling today?'

'Wretched,' he said, not even trying to smile.

'Well, I have brought you tea and milk toast. And there is a poultice for after.' She held out the bowl to him and readied the spoon.

He held out his hands for the tray. 'Really, Evelyn. While I appreciate your help, I can still manage to feed myself.' His voice was rough from the swelling of his throat, the words somewhat muffled by the difficulty of forming them.

'I see.' She would not be hurt by his tone. After the news he had received yesterday, it was perfectly natural that he would be short tempered. When she had returned to him, after talking with Sam, he had pretended to be asleep rather than acknowledge her presence.

She'd sat by him, until his breathing had become more regular and the play-acted slumber had become real. Then she'd continued to sit with him, enjoying the peace. She did not have the energy to argue with Sam again, nor did she particularly wish to speak with Michael. It felt good to sit, as the room grew dark, thinking nothing at all.

After, she had crept off to her room, not stopping to talk with Sam. She had not even summoned her maid, but had pulled off her dress and crawled beneath the covers to fall into a deep and troubled sleep. She had been up again at dawn, to prepare herself for another day of nursing.

But it seemed, if the patient could not avoid her by closing his eyes, he meant to bark at her until she left. 'Of course you can feed yourself,' she said with a smile. 'But I do not wish you to tire yourself.'

'Tire myself?' There was a pause that she suspected would have been a smothered oath from a man less patient than the Duke of St Aldric. 'You realise, Evelyn, that I have little to do all day but lie in bed, waiting for this complaint to pass.'

'And there is nothing more enervating than doing nothing at all,' she said firmly, thinking of how exhausting it was to sit quietly at his side and not give offence.

'Well, the least you could do is read to me from *The Times*,' he said. 'When I am well again, it will save me time in catching up.'

She adjusted his covers and laid a hand on his swollen cheek. 'I do not wish to upset you. I will ask Sam if it is all right.'

'By all means, ask Dr Hastings.' For the first time since she'd met him, Michael used a tone which was positively venomous.

Evie had to restrain herself from fussing with his covers again, trying to make up for her guilty memories. 'He is your physician,' she said as patiently as she could. 'Who else would I consult about anything that might affect your recovery?'

The duke sighed. 'I am sorry for being cross with you. You have done nothing to deserve it. It is the illness talking. I do not like idleness.'

'Really?' She smiled into her hand. 'I had not noticed.'

'And it bothers me to be dependent on Hastings.'

'We could get another doctor, if that is a problem.' Her father would welcome a chance to get Sam out of the house. And until she could find a way to break with Michael, it might be for the best not to have temptation continually in her path.

The duke shook his head. 'I cannot very well send him away, after making such a show of asking specifically for his help. He has made it plain that he does not want to associate with me. I am sure he cannot like the position I have forced him into. Much as I would wish to know him better, this situation is not making it easier on either of us.' But he looked quite morose at the thought of giving him up.

'He is a very independent man.'

'It is a family trait,' St Aldric agreed.

And so was this sense of noble self-sacrifice. Stubbornness as well, although she could not tell that to either man. 'Given time, you will overcome his resistance. I am sure that he is pleased to have found his roots, after all this time.' Secretly pleased, perhaps. He had not said any such thing to her. It felt strange that she could not be sure of his feelings. Though they had shared every secret in their young lives, he was hiding things from her now. It did not bode well for their future.

'I must trust your judgement, I suppose,' Michael said, with another sigh. 'You know him better than I.'

Now she was blushing. And she suspected he had noticed it. 'Do you wish anything more?'

She reached for the covers again, then stopped herself. There was a limit to the time she could spend smoothing a single sheet. 'Should I build up the fire?'

'Let it die down,' he said. 'It is too warm in here already. I am not chilled and you are becoming quite flushed.' His voice was all sympathy, providing this easy lie to cover her reactions.

It was just like him, worrying about another. It made her wish that she felt anything more than a wave of fondness to be treated so. 'Very well, then. As long as you are comfortable. Please, enjoy your breakfast.' How much pleasure he could get from it, she did not know. It was as bland and flavourless as her love for him, but he seemed to like that well enough.

'You needn't remain, if you don't wish to,' he added, picking up the spoon and managing a small bite. But she thought he looked rather depressed at the thought of being alone again.

For a moment, she almost forgot her resolve of the previous evening and blurted the truth. *I cannot stay. I am not worthy of your affection. And I do not love you back.*

But with his recovery just beginning, she did not want to do anything that might upset or weaken him. 'It is all right,' she said. 'I will stay as long as you need me.'

He looked up at her and smiled. 'Whatever would I do without you?'

And though her heart felt nothing but a combination of guilt and grim determination, she smiled back. Then she opened the book she had brought to entertain him and started to read.

When he began to doze, she marked the place and set the book at the bedside for later, then sat staring down at the sleeping man. Even with a swollen jaw, he was handsome. And today was the first time she'd heard a cross word from him. Considering the circumstances, it was not surprising. Even a saint might be cross, when ill and faced with the news that Sam had given him.

The Saint. His nickname suited him. He was not just a duke, he was a good man. He did not deserve this illness, or the possible consequences from it. Nor did he deserve to be shunned by his brother. At least, if she were here, he might never be alone again.

What would he do without her?

It was just one more thing that he never need find out.

Chapter Nineteen

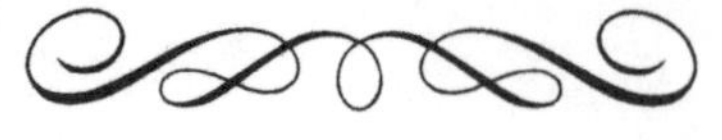

When Evie returned from the duke's room it was nearly lunchtime. Sam considered a second examination, but as if she could read his mind, Evie gave a single shake of her head.

'He is sleeping again. And he did not need the drugs for it. His forehead feels cooler and the swelling is coming down. He was able to manage his breakfast and nearly cleared the tray. All he needs right now is rest.'

Sam nodded. 'Your diagnosis is as good as mine, I suppose. If the symptoms are abating, I doubt I will need to bleed him. We will see what the day brings.'

He risked an encouraging smile. If St Aldric was on the mend, they might soon settle things between them. Although he dare not risk taking her back to bed, they might talk quietly for a while. He had not seen her since their argument yesterday. She would forgive him, if they could only be together. They had known each other for a lifetime and had loved almost that long. A week of disagreement would not separate them.

But now she paused in the doorway, neither advancing nor retreating. She just stood and watched him, without returning his smile.

He gestured to the chair opposite him. 'There is no reason why you cannot rest as well. He will be fine without you for a few hours. And you must take a bit of lunch. Your breakfast tray was untouched when Abbott came for it.'

'I was not hungry,' she said, still not moving.

'You are not taking ill, I hope,' he said, half-joking. 'If we are not careful, I will have to treat you as well.'

'No!' Her reaction was extreme and unexpected. She sounded almost as if she feared his touch.

He remembered how it had been for him, when he had wanted her and known it was impossible. The sight of her was agony and a touch was a cruel promise of a thing he would never have. 'I take it you have been thinking about what you must tell St Aldric.'

'I do not wish him to suffer more than he already has.'

'St Aldric, suffer?' Sam could not help the laugh. 'He is already healing. Two or three days of discomfort does not equate to suffering. If he thinks it so, then he does not know the meaning of the word.'

'You are being unfair to him,' Evie said.

She seemed to think he was cruel and not stating an obvious fact. 'You said yourself that he is better today.'

'But we will not know for some time if he will fully recover,' she said, still keeping her distance from him.

'Do you plan to remain silent until then? And I suppose that I am just to wait.' Sam gave an incredulous laugh. 'I wish you showed the same concern for my suffering as for his.'

'Six years passed with barely a word from you,' she said, shaking her head. 'And now, any delay is a trial?'

'Yes,' he said, for it was quite true. 'I am sorry that things were as they were. But that is past. We have waited long enough to be together.'

'We waited too long, I think. Now there is no future for us. I don't think there can be.' The playful and clever girl he remembered was gone. The woman standing before him was sadder and wiser than he'd ever wanted her to become. And he did not want to be the fault of it.

'What we have shared means nothing to you?'

'Of course it means something,' she said urgently. 'But meaning is not the same thing as promise. If you stay, we will go on as we have been. I cannot give myself fully to you because of my feelings for Michael. And you cannot give yourself completely to me, if you will not tell me the whole truth. We are at an impasse.'

Oath be damned. His mouth was already framing the truth, when he stopped himself. Just now, she claimed to have feelings for the duke. She had made her decision before speaking. What good would it do him to tell the truth, if she still did not want him?

If he told her everything, she would not thank

him for his honesty. It would destroy her faith in her father. She would see him as a sad wreck of a man, grasping at straws as she pushed him out of her life. And he would be throwing aside his promise to Thorne, as if his good name meant nothing to him.

He had thought he was a fiend who lusted for his sister. Instead, he had become the sort of monster who would seduce his brother's betrothed, destroy her family and promise anything to have his way.

The truth would hurt the woman he loved. He had sworn he would never do that. And if he broke that promise there was no point in living after.

'You are right, Evie,' he said, sad that the way forwards, now he'd found it, was so very empty. 'There is nothing to be done.'

'You must learn to call me Evelyn,' she reminded him. 'As everyone else does. We are grown now, you know. There is no place left for childish nicknames.'

'Of course, Evelyn.' *Evie*, his mind insisted.

She would never be Evelyn to him, no matter what his lips might say.

'It is for the best, you know.' Now that the moment was here, she was not angry. Nor did she seem relieved to be rid of him. There was only sorrow, as though she were mourning a death.

And he was still waiting for her to change her mind, like a prisoner hoping for reprieve. Had that been how she had felt, waiting for him to come home and not understanding the reason for his rejection? She had called to him, over and over, and he had refused her. But she had never given up trying to save him from himself.

Until now.

Really, what did he have to offer her? One hardly needed to be rescued from the fate that awaited her. In fact, he was recuing her now, just by leaving.

'We will see each other, of course, from time to time,' she allowed, offering a sop. 'It cannot be avoided. He is your only family, after all.'

You are my only family. And a few words of truth would destroy hers.

'You know that we will not,' he said, as gently

as possible. 'I will go, if that is really what you wish. But do not tell yourself that there will be any contact between us. I will not return. I could not bear to. And you must stop writing to me. This time, I will not read your letters.'

If the total and permanent loss of him bothered her, she did not say so. 'I have promised Father,' she said, insistently. 'And St Aldric, of course. I cannot go back on my word.'

But she could. They could run, right now, somewhere far away, where there would be no one to question them. 'They would understand.' In an instant, he imagined a whole life with her. And another. And another. And then he put them all aside as hopeless. Any choice required her co-operation. He had tried to win it and failed.

'It is you who must understand,' she said. 'I promised myself to a good man. He needs me. You know it is true. Set me free.'

His pain had no effect on her, now that she was resolved. She was as cold as he'd ever wanted to be, when he longed for her. Perhaps her affection was never more than a fleeting thing. But when they had lain together, it had seemed real enough.

'I know what is needed. I know what is required. And I know what people expect. But what do you want, Evie? What do *you* want?' For a moment, her eyes clouded and he was convinced that he could win her with reason.

'Was all your education for naught?' he said. 'You claimed an interest in medicine. There will be no place for it in the life you are choosing.'

And then he lost her again. 'Perhaps not. But, I will be able to accomplish much, as Duchess of St Aldric.'

'You want to do good?' he asked. 'You might help me in my work. We would do good together.' He imagined her, working at his side. He had thought it foolish at first. But now he could not imagine a better future.

She shook her head. 'It was a wonderful dream, Sam. But it was nothing more than that. It is time that I learned more conventional ways of helping others.'

'Without having to bloody your hands,' he said bitterly. 'I will not bother you again, Lady Evelyn. Not with my heart. Not with my work. And you can settle for your tepid marriage and your distant benevolence. I wish you well of it.'

'Next you will speak nonsense about differences in your ranks, or your not being good enough or rich enough for me.' Evie gave an exasperated sigh. 'In the end, the truth is this: St Aldric is honourable. He is truthful with me. You are not.'

And that was the rub. The one point he could not refute. St Aldric was a saint and above reproach. For all his arguments about the nobility of his love, Sam had bedded her the moment they were alone. And he could never, ever tell her the truth about the past. He would not change and she would not forgive.

He had lost. He had been so sure that, now he was free to marry her, it would all fall easily into place. He had forgotten to consider her feelings, her needs and her sense of justice, which was as strong as any man's. So much about her was strong. And it was all lost to him.

His skin went cold and the world had a distant, cotton-wrapped quality, as his brain tried to deny what he was hearing. Shock, he thought.

The prescription was brandy and lots of it. But that would be later, when he was away from her and not trying to salvage his pride. 'Very well, then,' he said. 'You must do as you promised, to St Aldric and to your father. Marry him. Be happy. Truly, that is what I wish for you. And that is a thing I cannot give.'

Chapter Twenty

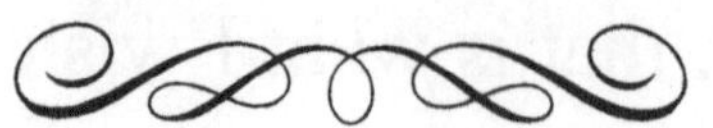

Sam neglected the afternoon examination of the patient, instead sending Evie, telling her to do whatever she felt was necessary to help her betrothed. She had returned to Michael, shortly after their conversation, taking her lunch with her so that she might share a meal with him.

Sam had eaten alone, in silence, wondering how long it would be until he could make a graceful exit from the house and the lives of the happy couple.

When he next saw the duke, it was well past supper. The man's condition all but answered the question.

'Doctor Hastings,' St Aldric said with a smile, sitting up further in the bed so they might talk eye to eye. 'How long do you mean to keep me here, now that I am recovering?' His voice was stronger and his colour better.

'Another week, at most,' Sam said. 'We must be sure that the last trace of illness is gone before you resume your regular duties.'

'I think I shall go mad, with another seven days of inactivity.'

'You shall have Lady Evelyn to keep you company,' Sam said, managing an ironic smile. 'But if you mean to descend into mania, I will leave the name of another physician who might help. A school friend of mine is now keeper at Bedlam. I am sure he will be glad of the change.'

'You will leave?' The duke raised his eyebrows. 'Are you trying to escape me again? I did not presume that this illness would convince you to accept my offer. But there is no need to run off to avoid me.'

'I am returning to sea,' Sam said. He was not yet sure if it was true. But neither did he care. His future did not really matter, now that he knew he would not share it with Evie.

'Don't be an idiot.' The duke was grinning at

him now, as if his life plans were all some enormous joke.

Sam kept his voice level. 'I understand the difference in our rank, your Grace—but I will not allow you to address me in that way.'

The smile disappeared. 'Devil take the difference in our rank, Sam. For just a moment, do me the kindness of remembering that we share a father, and that I am your elder by several months, and leave it at that. And I say you are an idiot if you stir from this place.'

Sam sighed and settled back in the chair at the bedside. 'If it will prevent you from agitating yourself, then very well, Michael.' The name felt odd on his tongue, but he forced it out. 'Say your piece.'

'We both know the reason you are leaving. It is Evelyn, is it not?' And now the duke pinned him to the spot with a glare. He had not seen the man use his rank in such a way. It was quite effective.

Sam weighed the possibility of lying, but only briefly. It seemed the Duke of St Aldric would not stand for prevarication. And if they were truly brothers, there ought to be some truth between them. 'Yes,' he said. 'It is because of Evelyn.'

'The solution is simple, then. I will retract my offer.'

'The hell you will.' He hoped that the new St Aldric liked the change in his demeanour. At the moment, he did not care that one must not dictate to a duke. 'Are you overcome with the idea that you can claim me as family? Biology does not give you a right to order my life for me. Or are you merely so caught up in your own rank that you think you can move people about like furniture? The honour of a lady is at stake and you will do nothing to compromise it.'

St Aldric laughed. 'I do not think the usual rules apply in this case. By giving her up, I would be doing her a service. She is staying with me out of pity. If there was the slightest chance of her heart breaking, you would be there to pick of the pieces, quick enough.'

'She would not have me.' Saying the words was like plunging into an ice bath. It was a brutal counter-shock to the numbness he had been feeling all afternoon. But it took some of the guilt away, so he continued, 'I tried. Heaven help me. I tried to take her from you. But she will not go. The breach between us is too great. I waited too long. And I have lost her trust.'

'I am sorry.' St Aldric settled back into the pillows again, looking as though he were the physician and Sam the patient.

'Don't be. She will forget me, once I am gone.'

'She belongs with you,' the duke reminded him, his voice patient and low.

'But she is better off with you.' Sam squared his shoulders and fiddled with the instruments on the table at his side, dropping them one by one into the bag on the floor. 'She will be a good wife, an excellent duchess. I wish you well. But you must understand if I do not stay for the wedding.'

'And this is how it must end, with all three of us being unhappy?'

'You? Unhappy?' Sam laughed, bitterly. 'The least you could do is take pleasure in your victory over me.'

'It was never my goal to be anyone's rival,' St Aldric said, with a shake of his head. 'I will do nothing to make Evelyn unhappy, for she is a sweet girl, and we could have done well together. But to find that I have family, only to lose it again?' He sighed. 'I cannot break with her and be an honourable man. And I cannot manage to keep you both.'

'That is the gist of it,' Sam agreed. 'At least, when you were at your weakest, I did not kill you. The thought crossed my mind. But I expect you know that.'

'I suppose I am glad that you resisted,' St Aldric replied. 'Although it might have been more of a mercy to finish me. If I am not to have an heir, there is little point in continuing.'

'Do not talk nonsense,' Sam said firmly, a doctor again. 'You have many years ahead of you. And I make no guarantees either for or against your chances of siring children.' Considering the extent of the illness, he was not optimistic. But anything was possible.

The duke was giving him a sympathetic smile again, as though he was the one to be offering comfort. 'You do not understand. I do not expcct you to.' He lifted the sheet and glanced down at his still-swollen body. Then he winced and dropped it again.

'It is better than it was yesterday,' Sam reminded him. 'You are healing. And it could have been worse,' he said, as encouragingly as possible. 'Men have died from this. Or been deafened. Or disfigured.'

'And I have been rendered impotent,' the duke snapped.

'We cannot be sure.'

'Until I have tried for years without success?' he said, sounding every bit as bitter as Sam felt. 'As everyone continues to remind me, I am a young man, with a long life ahead.'

'You are,' the doctor agreed.

'To what purpose is this long life I am to have? Am I to work for a lifetime, caring for my people and my land, only to leave it to no one? When I die, it will all fall to ruin.'

'You cannot know that.'

'The not knowing is likely to drive me mad,' his brother said, raking his hair with his hand. 'I will live. But St Aldric is as good as dead. And

I must watch all that my family has built, in the end of its days.'

'Our family,' Sam said, feeling the fleeting sense of kinship again.

'But in this you cannot help me,' St Aldric said, staring at the wall across the room. 'I am alone.'

'You have Evelyn.' Sam did his best to make his voice encouraging.

'God help her. This cannot be what she wished for.'

'You are a duke,' Sam reminded him.

'And less of a man than you.' Michael stared back at him. 'She loves you. Would you want to know that your wife will spend every moment of your marriage dreaming of another man?'

It was Sam's turn to look away.

'Do not bother to lie about it. If this is a day for difficult truths, what is one more? Will you have the courtesy to admit it?'

'What I want does not matter,' Sam said firmly. 'It is what she wants that matters. I never should have forgotten that. I handled things badly. Now, she has made her decision. She chose you.'

'Does she know the extent of my illness?'

'She read the medical books herself. It is the reason she will stay with you. She would not have you be alone.' Apparently, it did not matter how lonely Sam might be. 'If you break her heart over this, or disgrace her in any way, I will come back and take the life I have just saved.'

'Then God help us all,' St Aldric said, collapsing back on to the pillows.

'If this is an example of His mercy, I would prefer to do without it,' Sam said, dropping the last of the tools into his bag and closing it. 'And now, Michael, if you will excuse me? I think I shall go down to the port and wait for a high tide and a fresh wind.'

Chapter Twenty-One

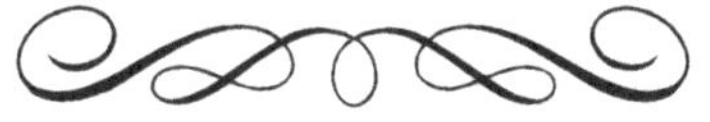

Sam was gone.

Eve had watched as he'd left the duke's room and walked past the sitting room without stopping. Shortly thereafter, she'd heard the slam of the door to the servants' stairway. And then she had seen no more of him.

She'd found a letter on the table, clearly outlining instructions for the duke's care, and what she should do if his condition changed for the worse. There were the names of several prominent physicians she might contact with problems. She could also contact them if St Aldric persisted in his desire for a personal doctor. If his condition devolved into sterility, as he feared, there might be some treatment for it that Sam had not learned. Other opinions might be sought.

It was everything she'd have hoped for from a truly dedicated doctor. And it was nice to know it came from Sam. Now that the decision had been made, he showed no jealousy and no desire for revenge. He wanted, above all, what was best for the patient. It seemed, in some things at least, he was exactly the man she'd have wished him to be.

But there was no word to her at all. Had she really expected a personal message, in a place where any might read it? An apology, perhaps. Or one last entreaty to change her mind and come to him. If he loved her, as he claimed, did she not deserve to know where he was going and what he was likely to do when he got there?

It was even worse than when he'd left the last time. Then she could at least write to him, even if he did not answer. This time, she had told him she did not care. And he had removed the temptation to change her mind, by making it impossible to do so.

It was just as well. When it came to Sam, she was no better than the Biblical Eve. She resisted now. But at some point, all her noble plans to be loyal to the duke would fail her. She would weaken and run back to Sam. But if she was married, they could not allow it to. He had severed the link between them with surgical precision.

It had been the right thing to do. Michael was her choice. Given the way things had turned out, he was the only choice she ever should have made. Their love might be a pale imitation of the kind she had hoped for, but he needed her in a way that Sam never had.

Sam was gone and she was alone. But that meant that the responsibility for the care of the duke fell to her. So she did as Sam would have done and made sure that the patient was settled for the night, offering medications that were refused as no longer necessary and refilling the glass at bedside with fresh, cool water. Then she had left him in peace until morning.

Tonight, she did not return to her room. Instead, she slept uneasily in the bed that she had shared with Sam. One of the housemaids had been deemed immune, having suffered through the mumps a year or two before, and was allowed limited access to the third floor, to provide the necessary cleaning. She must have visited here, for the sheets had been changed and the bed made up properly. There was no trace of what they had done there in anything but Eve's memory.

The next morning, before ringing for breakfast, she washed and dressed herself, taking special care with her appearance, so that she might be a pleasant sight for her betrothed. Then she went to the end of the hall to receive the tray from Abbott, approving the contents. They were hardly a proper English breakfast, but were they were much less bland than the day before.

Then she knocked once and entered the duke's room with a serene smile, sure that no trace of her heavy heart would be apparent to him. 'Good morning, Michael. I have brought you your porridge.' She set the tray down where he could reach it. 'There is the cream for it. Honey as well. And a nice cup of coffee.' She fell silent, reminding herself that, since the illness had not rendered him a blind, deaf, idiot, she did not need to recite the menu.

'Evelyn.' He sounded tired and she put her hand on his, willing strength into him.

'You are doing much better today. I can see the difference.' The illness was abating. The swelling had reduced much from the previous day. But he looked grey, as though he had not slept well. She hoped that this was not a sign of relapse, but merely proof that fighting the infection had tired him.

'That is good to know,' he said. 'But where is my brother physician, so that I may thank him for it?' There was a kind of dryness in the statement, as though there might be some irony in offering those thanks.

'He…is gone.' She swallowed, unsure of what to say. 'I shall be both doctor and nurse to you now.' She gave another artificially bright smile, hoping that this would be sufficient for an explanation.

'Why this sudden change in plans?' Michael asked, still expressionless. 'I assumed he would stay with us through the wedding, at least.'

'He does not like to stay too long in any one place.' It might even be the truth. She had not known the adult Sam long enough to ask his opinion. 'I believe his intention was to go back to the navy.'

'Then he is a fool.' St Aldric offered no other explanation for this.

'You need not worry. He assured me, before he left, that you were all but mended and that I would have no trouble tending you from this point.'

'Did he?'

'Yes.' She nodded eagerly. Too eagerly perhaps, for he was staring at her with the same ironic expression he had used at the news of his doctor's departure.

He was focused on her now. And for a moment, she felt that she was truly in the presence of a duke and not some handsome but powerful friend. 'And did he inform you of the likely result from this illness? He assured me you knew, but I would like to hear it from your lips as well.'

'That you might be unable to father children?' She put off the smile and made sure that she did not stammer over the words, for it would only make them worse. She must be as stoic as Sam would have been, when sharing an unfavourable diagnosis. 'Yes, I am aware. But we cannot know for sure until we have tried.'

'You mean, when we have married,' he said patiently.

'Of course.' That was what she should have said. Now he might think she knew far too much about the process. She should be innocent, and ignorant, if she was to carry on with this farce.

And it was wrong of her to think of her impending marriage to the Duke of St Aldric as a farce. It was an honour. All the more so because he needed her.

The silence between them had carried on far too long. What was she to say next? Or should she pretend that it was a comfortable thing between two people who would be so close as not to be bothered by a little quiet?

'And you are all right with this?' The duke chose not to notice the awkward moment. 'It means you might never have children. I should have thought, with your interest in midwifing, that you would want to be a mother.'

'Of course,' she said. 'But I am also aware that

we do not always get what we might want in life.' Right now, she must not be thinking of Sam.

'And next you will tell me that Man proposes, but God disposes.' He waved a hand. 'Pray, do not bother.' Was it her ears, or did he actually sound cynical? He had been ill, of course. And at the moment, he was under much stress. But it was still most unlike him.

'That has ever been the case,' she said. 'It was thus, even before you became ill. We might never have had children. Though we are young and strong, we have no guarantee of longevity. There is simply no knowing the future.'

'Carpe diem,' he muttered, pushing his untouched breakfast aside. 'But that does not change my need for an heir. In fact, it increases it. If I die tomorrow, my life would have had no meaning.'

'Of course it would,' Eve said, patting his hand.

She was patting his hand again. She must stop it, or he would think she could manage nothing more than the platonic affection she might shower on any invalid. 'You are a great man, Michael. And no matter what happens, people will remember you as such.'

'They would remember me as the last St Aldric,' he reminded her. 'And I would have failed my family in the one thing that should have been simple.' He gave her another sharp look. 'If you had given me your answer when I'd first asked for it, we'd have been married by now. This might never have been a concern.'

Now, he would turn his unhappiness on her. She wanted to argue that it was hardly her fault. There was no way she might have known the future and the results of her decisions. But it was true. She had hesitated when he needed her to be decisive. And it must never happen again. 'I'm sorry,' she replied.

'Sorry does not change the fact that I need an heir.' At one time, he had said that he needed a wife. But that had never been what he'd meant. Circumstances were forcing the truth from him. But she had told Sam she wanted the truth, even if it was unpleasant. She had no right to complain when she received it.

'There is a way that we might be sure of progeny,' the duke said, slowly and carefully. 'But it would require a sacrifice on your part.'

'Of course,' she said, giving his hand an encouraging squeeze. She owed him her loyalty now, if only to make up for the times that she had wavered.

'I must have a son. A legitimate heir. And that might be quite beyond me.'

He was staring at her as though she would be the key to it. But there was nothing she could do to alter the course of his illness. He must mean something quite different. 'Are you suggesting we perpetrate a ruse of some kind?'

'In a way,' he said cautiously. 'I did not sleep last night, trying to find another way. But I could think of none but this: you must appear to be pregnant with my child.'

'If we went away for a time, and returned with an infant…'

He shook his head. 'People would wonder. But if they saw that you were carrying a child, and if I acknowledged it as mine, they would not dare to question us. They would announce us fortunate. All gossip would be silenced.'

'But how…?' The answer was simple, of course. But he could not possibly be suggesting it.

'If you were to lie with a man not unlike me in appearance. Someone as alike as a brother…'

She already had. And she had promised herself that it would never happen again. 'I will not be unfaithful to you,' she said, setting the temptation as far from herself as she could.

'It is not infidelity if it is agreed upon by both parties.' He was looking at her without emotion, as though she was worth nothing more to him than the child she might produce.

'And our marriage vows mean nothing to you?'

'I will fulfil my part in them,' he said solemnly. 'But as I remember your part, you would be called to obedience.'

Sit quietly. Have no opinion other than the weather. Play with your kitten and do not think too hard, or speak too loudly. And now, this. 'What you are suggesting is horrible.' She dropped his hand. 'I will not hear it.'

'Not this year, perhaps.' His face was positively grim. 'But as time passes, and we do not have a son, you might feel differently. And I? I would insist.'

'You would require me to do something so repellent?'

'As to make you seduce the man you have loved for years?' Now he laughed and the cynicism was obvious. 'My half-brother would be the perfect candidate. I suspect, after a few more years at sea, he would be all too willing to bed you, should you tell him tales of your unhappiness with me. I have seen the two of you together and the way you look at each other, when you think no one might notice. He was a fool for not taking you from me, when he had the chance.'

'You knew?' It was pointless to lie, now that it was too late to matter.

He nodded. 'I knew from the first day that I would never have all of your heart. But it was not your heart that was required. I would have had no objection to a dalliance, once your obligation to me was fulfilled. But this solution will work just as well.'

She had thought him good, almost beyond belief. And she had berated herself for betraying him. But now she could hardly bare to look at him. 'How could you?'

'Easily, I assure you. Because it needs to be done. Think of it as one more duty that you will face if you truly wish to marry me. For you see, my dear, being a duchess is sometimes quite different than being a lady.'

'But when you offered, I thought…'

'That I loved you?' His smile, which had seemed to be benevolent, was really no better than patronising. 'At any time, have I attempted to mislead you? I did not make my offer out of love, nor did I flatter myself in believing that you accepted it for that reason. We are fond of each other. But it would be a lie to claim that it is more than that. The marriage was expedient for both of us. And expediency might demand the situation that I describe to you now. While I appreciate your willingness to stand by me in the face of adversity, this marriage is likely to require more from you than pity. Do you still wish to stay?'

'No.' Tears were slipping down her nose, and she wiped them away with the back of her hand. She should be strong enough to do this. Or she should at least have stopped to think through her answer. But there was no other answer she could make. 'I am sorry. If this is our future, I cannot marry you.'

Now he was patting her hand with the same sort of benign sympathy that she had offered him. 'I thought not. It is a shame, for I am sure we would have been a great success.'

'You are not angry?' He seemed almost relieved. Since she was as well, she could not bring herself to feel insulted.

'I am angry about many things, my dear. But not at you. You love my brother. He loves you. Go to him. Be happy.' St Aldric was giving her an exhausted attempt at a smile, as though he had completed some onerous but necessary task. 'And now, if you will forgive me, I wish to rest.' He turned away from her, face to the wall and sighed.

She reached out a hand and touched his hair, then she withdrew. She had no right. It was over between them.

If it gave him comfort, as it seemed to, then let the duke think that she was going to Sam. But she could not manage that, either. Her freedom did not remove the sting of knowing that he had waited too long to declare. Would he still want her, now that Michael did not? If this sudden love for her was anything more than jealousy towards his brother, he should have told her so when she'd asked.

If there was another motive for avoiding her and spurning her offers, and the sudden, convenient return of his love, he had said nothing about it. While she did not wish to believe the worst, she could find nothing else that made sense.

Chapter Twenty-Two

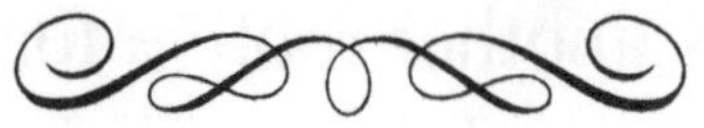

Walking to the study was like going from the sick room to a funeral. That would be what it would seem to her father, who viewed her impending marriage almost as though it were a live thing. And she had not just witnessed the death of it, she had been instrumental in bringing it about.

She had murdered her one chance at a title and a life of ease. No one would want a girl who jilted the most eligible bachelor in London. How picky must she be, if even a saint was not good enough for her?

Yet she felt almost happy to be free of it. She had parted from him as a friend. She would not have to lie to St Aldric about her feelings, since he understood them already. She would not have to stifle herself and conform to his ideals for a perfect wife. She could go on much as she'd been living it, lonely, but with time to study and to help the women in the villages around their country home.

But it would take all of her charm to persuade Father that this was for the best. She would kiss his temples and assure him that there would be no problem with the duke. They would still be welcome in his home and he in theirs. Their household was well managed now. But it would continue to be so if she remained as a spinster in his house. She could care for him in his dotage.

The future, while it was not rosy, was solid and comfortable. Once he was over his disappointment, he would see the advantages of her staying. She would run the house for him, as she had. And she would always be his loving and devoted daughter.

Even if she could not have Sam it was better to live this way. She might be alone, but at least she was not living under the misapprehension that love would come to her. The past was dead. Memories were illusions. And even saints had feet of clay.

Now that she had arrived at it, she hesitated in the open door of the study. She felt like a very small girl again, wanting to see her parent, but afraid to interrupt his important business.

And, just as he always had, he looked up and smiled at her, as though she was the light of his life. 'Evelyn. Come.' He put up a hand, curling a coaxing finger. 'Doctor Hastings has finally freed you from your duties, so that you might visit me?'

'Father.' Her tongue was all but sticking in her mouth. *I have done a horrible thing.* She had not, really. She had done the only thing possible. But how to explain it?

He saw her distress and held out his arms to her, and she went into them without question, drawing strength from his embrace.

'Does something upset you?' He held her away from him.

'Sam has gone,' she said. And for the first time that day she felt like crying.

'You knew he would,' her father said, unaffected. 'At best, he might have stayed through the wedding. But he has not been a constant friend, has he? He all but disappeared from your life for years. Now that he is back in London, I am surprised that he stayed as long as he did. But I suspect that was caused by nothing more than the duke's illness.'

'Father!' Now of all times, he seemed full of his old grudge against a man who could do him no real harm. 'Sam's going is neither here nor there. He can do as he wishes, for he is a free man.'

'Then what is troubling you, my dear? It is not St Aldric, is it? Hastings assured me that the man would make a recovery. Not complete, perhaps. But it has turned out as well as can be expected.'

'He is fine,' she agreed, after a steadying breath. 'As fine as one could hope to be, after a severe illness. He grows stronger by the hour. But he is in low spirits.'

'Ahh. Yes.' Her father took an equally steadying breath. He was obviously aware of what this particular illness might mean, but did not want to talk about such a sensitive matter with his daughter. 'Well, there is nothing to be done about the past and no predicting the future.'

'I tried to tell him so. But he would not listen.'

'He will come around in time,' her father insisted.

'Perhaps,' she agreed. 'But he was saying things today that could not be forgiven or forgotten. And it is quite clear that he never loved me.'

Her father laughed dismissively. 'That is hardly a problem, I am sure. He is a good man. He is fond of you. That is enough.'

'Not to me,' she said. 'At one time, I thought so. But truly, it is not. And I told him so.'

'I beg your pardon. But I could not have heard you correctly.' Her father put his hand to his ear, feigning deafness to give her time to correct her last statement. 'You do not argue with a duke, Evelyn, no matter how *outré* his behaviour becomes.'

'His behaviour was not *outré*,' she said, equally incredulous that her father would support the opposite side in any argument she might have. 'The things he said…' How much did she want to tell him of the suggestions made? 'Let me simply say that they could not be attributed to eccentricity. He proposed that we have a marriage so far outside the bounds of propriety that I told him

I wanted no part in it. I asked for my freedom. He gave it to me. We have agreed to end our engagement.'

Her father was slack jawed in amazement, before sputtering, 'Wh-wh-whatever you said to him to cause this separation, you must go back immediately and unsay it,'

As though there would be any going back. 'Certainly not. I am sorry, Father, but our conversation resulted from something he said to me. I had done nothing to provoke him.'

'Then perhaps it was a result of his illness,' her father said, voicing one last hope. 'He will be better in a week. When he is, he will apologise to you. All will be well again.'

'It was not the illness talking,' she said patiently. 'He is very nearly healed. But the possible repercussions gave us reason to discuss the future. We simply agreed that the proposed union would make neither of us happy and dissolved it. We are still on good terms. But we will not marry.'

'And what are you to do now?' her father moaned, his head in his hands. 'And do not tell me that it is a disagreement over Hastings. If he is gone again, he will not be able to interfere.'

'No, Father, I can honestly say that it is not. The difficulty lies between Michael and myself. I cannot tell you more than that.' She came around to the other side of the desk and hugged him, to prove that her love for him had not changed at all.

His arm came up to pat her on the shoulder as well. 'All the same, you might well have ruined your only chance at happiness. Who will have you, now?'

'You needn't worry,' she said, smiling now to show him that her heart was not the least bit broken. 'Not about anything at all. I am going to stay here with you. I am sure you would have missed me terribly, had I left you. But now I shall be here always, to care for you.'

'I am not yet so old that I need a nurse,' her father said sharply and withdrew his arm.

'I know that, Father,' she said. 'But you must admit, my housekeeping skills have been useful thus far. I still cannot sew a straight seam, of course. But I manage the servants well enough, don't I? Your home is as you like it. I will see that it remains so.'

Then he cleared his throat, as though preparing to broach some awkward news. 'The truth is, my dear, I had plans of a matrimonial nature myself. There is a widow that I am quite fond of. But now that you plan to remain…'

She had been prepared for anger. Perhaps some threat of punishment that she would easily avoid. But this reaction was totally unexpected. Her own father did not want her to stay. In fact, he had been in the process of disposing of her, to make way for another, and she had spoiled everything. She sat down with a thump on the chair by the desk, momentarily unable to support her own weight.

'Do not worry, my dear,' he said with the same reassuring smile she had planned to use on him. 'I am sure, if we make an effort, we will think of someone to take you. And we must look on the bright side. You may have lost the duke. But at least Hastings is gone again. We are most fortunate to be rid of him.'

Here again was his strange dislike for Sam,

who had been as close to him as a son, almost since birth.

'But I doubt his family will see him, either,' she said. 'He refused the position that St Aldric offered him. And at the time of his parting, they were still no closer to behaving as brothers should.'

'You are too soft hearted by half, Evelyn,' he said, smiling at her with some of the fatherly warmth she had expected. 'In the end, they will both be better off if he returns to sea.'

'I hope he does not,' she said. No matter what had happened, she did not wish him ill. 'It is far too dangerous. I have told him so, but I do not think he listened.'

'Not so dangerous as it might have been, had he remained ashore.' Her father glanced at the door, as though wanting to make sure that there was no one in the hall who might hear. 'I have known, my dear, of your affection for him. It simply would not do. Some day you will see the wisdom of it and accept that it was not meant to be. If you ever wish to marry well, Samuel Hastings must not hang over the union like a cloud.'

'He would do nothing to hurt me,' she said. He had hurt her already. But no one would know about that.

'He would not be able to help himself,' her father said, with a sad shake of his head. 'He would always be searching for some sign of dissatisfaction between you and your husband.'

It was almost as St Aldric had described it, with Sam waiting in the wings for her first sign of weakness. But hadn't that been exactly what had happened already? She would not be sure for several weeks that she had not made a horrible mistake that might leave her running back to the duke and agreeing to his original plan of providing an heir in any way possible. 'Well, I am not to marry St Aldric now, so that hardly seems a problem.'

'It is even worse, my dear,' her father said, almost wringing his hands with agitation. 'If you do not find another suitor, there will be nothing left to curb his acting on the impulse to offer comfort that you would not need.'

'He needed no curbing in the past. He left easily enough, the first time, and we have hardly seen him for six years.' This time, he'd been old enough to satisfy his lust. Once that had been done he'd left again, without so much as a thought to the possibility of issue.

'That was a different thing entirely,' her father said, with a resolute nod, as though the past was settled. 'It took considerable effort on my part to get him away from you.'

She could not have heard it right. Sam had said nothing of her father, in any of this. If he was not at fault, then why had he not said so? 'You were the reason for his departure,' she said, hoping that he would correct himself.

Her father looked embarrassed. 'It was well past time that you were separated. He had been too long in your company and had grown over-fond of you.'

'He loved me,' she said, half-believing it.

'But not as he should have,' her father corrected. 'Not as I intended.'

'You intended that we love each other?' she said, still confused.

'As brother and sister. But certainly nothing more than that.' And now her father looked incensed. 'The foolish boy actually came to me, ready to offer for you before you were out. He seemed to hope that, by making his intentions clear, you could be encouraged to wait for him. I told him it was impossible, of course.'

It had not been impossible. Not at all. She had waited as long as she could, even without his offer. 'You refused him and then he left,' she said. Sam had mentioned nothing of the offer, probably unwilling to admit to his early weakness at taking whatever bribe her father had offered.

'Not at first. He was just as stubborn as he is now. It might be an admirable quality, when one is without family and must make one's own way in the world. But not when it set his sights on something that he could never have.' Her father gave a little shake of the head and a rueful smile. 'Imagine, my dear, being married to someone with no name to call his own and in trade.'

'He is a physician,' she corrected. 'It is not so very poor a choice, if a gentleman must take employment. And it certainly would not matter, had there been love between us.'

'Of course it would have mattered,' her father

said with exasperation. 'There would be no rank, less money and a house not so fine as the one you live in now. And certainly no bevy of servants bowing and scraping and calling you "your Grace."'

'I never asked for any of those things,' she said quietly, wondering if that was what Sam had thought when he'd first gone.

'But you deserve them, all the same,' he said. 'You are my only daughter, my one dear child. And I will have nothing less for you than a titled husband and a life free from worry. Sam Hastings could not offer that. Thus it was necessary for him to leave.'

'So Sam thought me too far above him?'

'On the contrary. He insisted that it would spur him to even greater success, to keep you in luxury. He would find a way to provide for you, no matter the risk.'

'And yet he went away.' And proved that it was all nothing but talk.

'Not easily,' her father replied. 'No matter my arguments, he would not be dissuaded. I threatened to cut him off without a cent. He did not care. I offered him money to leave. He would not hear of it.'

Eve's heart grew full at the thought of the young Sam arguing ardently for her hand. He'd claimed to love her. And it must have been true. What reason could her father have to lie about such things, when it was clear that he held Sam in contempt? 'And what happened then?'

'He threatened to put the idea to you. If I did not agree, the two of you would run off and be married in Scotland. Would it not be more respectable to bind you to him in betrothal? Then the pair of you would wait until he had established himself in business before seeking marriage.' Her father gave a huff of disgust. 'It was blackmail, pure and simple. He was toying with your reputation. I could not let it stand.'

But Sam's argument sounded quite reasonable to her. It had been what she wanted. Even if her father had denied it, Sam should have put the suggestion to her. 'Why did he not run off with me, as he promised?'

'He would have, had I not offered an argument he could not refute.' Her father took a breath, then froze up, as if realising that he had spoken too much. 'And the rest is nothing for delicate ears to hear, my dear.'

Even after six years, Sam must have felt the same, for he would not speak, even if she thought ill of him. Whatever had been said clearly involved her, yet no one would do her the courtesy of sharing the secret that had altered the course of her whole life. She dropped her argument and smiled knowingly. 'You needn't bother to protect me, Father. He told me everything before he left.'

'He told you!' Her father's voice was thunderous and he rose and slammed his fist down on the desk for emphasis. 'That was between him and me and should have passed no further. He is a bounder and a cad. A viper in the bosom of this family. And if he would tell you such a thing, it proves everything I suspected about him. Blood will tell, Evelyn. Blood will tell.'

'His father was a duke,' she said softly.

'And his mother was a…seamstress,' he finished, as though narrowly avoiding yet another word that was not suitable for her ears. 'His revelation was nothing more than an attempt to turn you against me.'

'And that is why you must tell me your side of it,' she said, coaxing a little bit more of the truth. 'So that I might understand the whole.'

'I had promised to protect him,' her father said, 'and raise him as my own. But there are limits to what a man will do for a friend, even when that friend is a duke. I had never promised that he should marry my daughter. I am sure old St Aldric would not have expected that from me.'

Now old St Aldric's opinion counted above hers. Were dead men allowed to make up her mind for her as well? 'He could not have known what would happen,' she said, leaving the door open for more information.

'I could not tell him his father's name.' Her father could hardly meet her eyes. 'But that did not mean that I could not tell him that there was a good reason I had raised him. And that his parentage would require that the two of you never marry.'

'What difference could his true father have made in that?' But he had not known about the duke until just recently. Before that, he must have assumed he knew his origins and that they prevented him from marrying. It was only when he learned the truth that he was free to come to her.

A horrible thought occurred to her. *Oh, please, let it not be so.* 'What did you tell him, Father?' She took him by the arm and shook it, as if she could rattle the information from him, praying all the while that it was not as she suspected. 'What did you say?'

'I told him that he had mistaken the natural affinity of a brother and sister for something different. That the bond between you was an affection arising from blood and kinship. His confusion was unfortunate, but that he must see a marriage between the two of you would be against the laws of God and man.'

'You told him…' The truth surged in her stomach, so suddenly that she felt unwell.

'I told him that I had raised him like a son because that was what he was.' Her father looked embarrassed. 'And really, he was as much a son as I would ever have. It was not a complete lie. Merely an exaggeration.'

'And he left because he thought...' She gave a shudder of distaste and remembered his reactions in his rooms, and in the garden. His frenzied kisses, revulsion at his own weakness and his vow that there could never be anything between them.

The night of her engagement, the impediment had been lifted. And he had come to her immediately, a changed man.

Her father was still speaking. 'It was the only way I could think of to part the two of you. You had been as thick as thieves, for years. He had all but worshipped you, since the moment of your birth. But you must see that it could not have been...' The words were rushing out of him, as though a complete explanation would make them sound less heartless.

My poor dear Sam... It all made sense, now. His obvious attraction to her. His sudden disappearance. And his insistence that he felt nothing honourable. And now that he was free, she had chosen another and forced him away.

She rose from the chair and took a staggering step away from her father. It was like backing away from the life she had always thought was hers. She had never doubted his love. But she saw her own life, clearly, for the first time. He had kept her, like a plant in a sunless room, not noticing as her dreams had withered. He had thought he was protecting her, but instead he had been protecting his plans for her.

'I had to do it.' Her father held out a hand to her, as though trying to draw her back to his side. 'Do you not understand?'

'It is over now, Father.'

'Because he is gone.'

She shook her head. 'Because you cannot lie to us, ever again. If you love me as you say, then it must be the truth between us, always and for ever. Or you will lose me, just as you have lost Sam.'

But this time, she had been the one to lose Sam. She had sent him away. He had left without a word and she had no idea where to seek him. She turned, looking wildly around her, but knowing that there would be no clue. She looked to her father, who could no longer be trusted, even if help was offered. Then she thought of the one person who she could trust, though no sane person would dare to ask him for help in such a matter.

'Evelyn, wait!'

But the voice was already behind her and becoming fainter as she ran down the hall. She had not a moment to lose. She had waited too long already. She ran to the stairs and up the next two flights, chest tight from the mix of exertion and anxiety. She took only a moment to compose herself, before bursting into the sick room.

St Aldric looked up at her entrance with a benign smile. He was sitting up in bed and the morning papers were spread about him on the bedclothes.

The thought flitted through her mind that she should scold him for overexerting himself, then she remembered that she had no right to do so, especially not after the discussion they'd had only moments ago. If she was no longer welcome in the room, her advice would be even less so. Unsure how to begin, her knees bent, her head bowed and she whispered a breathless, 'Your Grace...'

'Don't talk rot, Evelyn.' He pushed the paper aside and gestured to the chair at his bedside.

She took it. 'I was afraid, that you would not wish to see me, after…'

'Your perfectly reasonable request that we dissolve our engagement?' If the parting bothered him, there was very little evidence of it. The slightly strained look at the corners of his eyes, perhaps. Or the faint crease in his brow. Vanity would demand her to be hurt by his indifference. But Eve could not manage to be other than relieved.

'I need your help,' she blurted. 'I have made a mistake.'

'Only one?' He was still smiling. 'Of course I shall help you. Unless you mean to come back to me, Evelyn. I am afraid I will not take you.'

That was almost insulting, yet she still did not care. She smiled back at him. 'I need to find Sam.'

Now the duke beamed at her. 'I was hoping you would say such. His plan is to return to the sea.'

'He promised me he would not.' She had been praying it would be Scotland. Or some other landlocked place that he might easily be retrieved from. But suppose he had gone with the morning tide?

'He promised you?' The duke gave a short laugh. 'He would break that promise, then, as quickly as he was able.'

'Why…?'

'When a man loses all he values, Evelyn, he is likely to do the most foolish and self-destructive thing he can imagine. You were the reason he went to sea before. And you are the reason he will return to it.'

It was so clear now. So simple. Why had she not understood? 'But how will I find him?' Three-quarters of the globe was water. And he sought to be lost.

The duke plucked a page off the bed sheets and thrust it at her. It was the shipping news, with a neat schedule of tides, arrivals and departures. He pointed. 'That one.'

'How can you be sure?'

'It is bound for Jamaica. Distant, dangerous and deficient in English women. That is the one he will choose. Africa would be better, of course.

But it is damnable weather to go 'round the horn at this time of year. Most ships' captains are not nearly so suicidal as our Samuel is likely to be.'

'Suicidal?' She had imagined him to be adventurous, not fatalistic.

'It is why you must waste no time in retrieving him.' He handed her a note, pencilled in a shaky but legible hand on the flyleaf of the book she had been reading him. 'Give this to my groom and say that you must borrow my carriage. The crest on the door is very handy for moving crowds and loosening tongues.' Then he turned from her again, gathering up the papers to read.

Chapter Twenty-Three

Sam sat at breakfast in the public room of his inn, trying not to think about the past, though everything seemed to remind him of it. The chops and ale in front of him were a solid replacement for the shirred eggs, toast and kippers that he had eaten yesterday. The food at the Thorne town house had been as good as he remembered.

He did not want to remember.

He stared fixedly at the food in front of him.

Beer for breakfast had an unapologetically masculine feel to it. It was fortifying, as was the chop. It settled the liquor, which still sloshed in his stomach, after a drunken evening. If he meant to walk the docks searching for an outbound ship, he would need energy. He finished the last of the meat on his plate and paid the innkeeper for the meal and another day's lodging. And then he went to seek his fortune.

The Port of London was full of merchantmen. Stevedores hauled bales and barrels up and down the gangplanks and up the dock towards warehouses. Nearby, he could smell tobacco and salted fish. There would be cotton as well, and wool woven and ready for export.

The bustle of commerce was interesting. But life on such a ship would not be. And what need would any of these captains have for a doctor? While he could not say he wished for Napoleon to escape again, a lasting peace would render him unnecessary.

Unwanted. Extraneous. Unloved. There were so many words to describe him now. It had been a point of pride that, if nothing else, he was useful member of society. But the previous two weeks had left him feeling spent. He had nothing left to give. At least, he had nothing that anyone wanted.

The docks of the East India Trading Company were more compelling. They still stank of fish and sailors, but the undercurrent of spice and tea stirred his lethargic spirit. Perhaps he would not bother with doctoring. He could be an adventurer. If he liked Asia, he could settle there. There would be no shortage of disease in a tropical climate.

But perhaps the Dutch merchantman moored ahead would be better. Sugar cane and rum in the Caribbean. It might be less expensive to stay drunk when the supply was so near. And treating lepers was so selfless that he might compete with dear Michael for his sainthood.

One thought of his brother brought all the memories of Evie rushing back. He had told her he would not go to sea. It frightened her. Surely the events that had followed would exempt him from any promises made. And if he went to Edinburgh, he might see something about St Aldric and his duchess in the papers from time to time. He would lack the strength to ignore it and would tear the old wounds open again thinking of her.

'Sam!'

He was thinking of her now, when he had promised himself he would not. The memories were so vivid that he could almost hear her voice. But these waking dreams were tame compared to what he saw whenever he closed his eyes. Perhaps he could find a way to do without sleep. Or else he would lie down some night to dream of her and never wake up again.

'Sam Hastings!'

That was not a dream. That was a real voice. But what would Evelyn Thorne be doing on the docks? He turned to look in the direction of the sound and saw the St Aldric carriage parked, in all its gleaming glory, and a liveried footman reaching to open the door.

Sam stumbled backwards into a passing navvy who swore and pushed him aside, but he hardly noticed. He could not see her. Not now. Not when he was so close to escape. And certainly not when she was rigged out as the damned Duchess of blasted St Aldric.

He had an insane desire to laugh. It seemed that, the closer he got to sea, the more his manners deteriorated. And it also seemed that he might have to jump from the dock and swim for India if he meant to get away from Evelyn Thorne. She was on the ground and running towards him, blocking his escape. It hardly mattered. The sight of her had frozen him to the spot like a statue.

'Ev-hhhh.' Her body hit his with no small force, knocking the air from his lungs. He tried desperately to catch his breath, but the mouth that covered his made it all the more difficult. His gasp brought her tongue into his mouth, and the need to trap it there and keep it for ever superseded anything so common and mortal as respiration.

He was breathless and lightheaded. If he could not manage to fill his lungs, he would black out and fall into the river. But he was being kissed by Evie and nothing else mattered. Her hands were around his waist, stroking his back to ease the tightness in his chest. And with each breath she took, she gave life back to him. She was air, and water, and sunshine. She was food and drink. She was everything he needed to survive.

He held her to him, so tightly that heaven and earth could not part them. She fit so perfectly in his arms, as if she was designed to complement him. No other woman had ever felt like this. No one ever would. No one but his Evie.

She leaned away for a moment and stared up

at him, blue eyes wide and full of mischief. He ought to tell her that it was disquieting to have her kiss with her eyes open. But there was no changing Evelyn Thorne, once she had an idea in her head. He had best get used to it.

'I have found you,' she said proudly.

'You have,' he agreed. But why had she found him? Was this just another attempt to argue with him? Would it lead to another goodbye? He doubted his heart could stand that.

'I worried that I had lost you, when you were not at the inn. But the footman said your chest was there and I did not think you would leave without it.'

'True,' he said, hoping that this was not a prelude to another rejection.

She sniffed. 'You smell like beer.'

'Breakfast,' he said.

'And medicine.' She put her nose to his lapel. 'We must have this coat cleaned immediately, so that you make a better impression on patients.'

We? That sounded wonderfully possessive. But he must take nothing for granted. 'Evelyn?' He pushed her away so that he could think clearly enough to speak an entire sentence. 'Why are you here?'

'I came for you.'

What a beautiful sound that was. Almost as good as *I love you*. But it could have other meanings than the one he wanted to give to it. 'There is nothing wrong with the duke, I trust?' he asked cautiously and braced himself for the worst.

'Other than that I do not love him and he does not love me?' She smiled. 'No. There is nothing wrong with him at all.' She gave him another small kiss on the corner of his mouth.

For a moment he could not breathe again. And then he sighed like the lovesick fool he was.

She was staring at his lips, as though admiring the shape of them, and touched the lower one with the tip of her finger. 'The engagement is over. I parted on good terms with St Aldric. We are still friends. He loaned me his carriage and told me how to find you. And you must promise to be his friend as well. He needs friends, you see.'

'Yes, Evelyn.' He hardly cared what he was promising, so entrancing was the thought of that fingertip, just out of reach. He moved his mouth to catch it, nipping it lightly, sucking it into his mouth.

They were kissing on a dock and he could hear the distant jeers of passing seamen. The suggestions they were making were crude and vulgar. And, praise heaven, for the first time in his life, some of them were in the realm of possibility. He needed to get her away from here, to get her alone. And to get her undressed. And he needed it soon.

She pulled her finger away and gave him the lightest slap on the cheek to punish him, then let her palm rest there and dropped her head to his chest. 'Afterwards, I talked to Father.' There was no playfulness in her voice now. She sounded hesitant, and as shaken as he did when thinking of his conversations with Thorne.

He sobered. 'I see.' She had not been spared, after all. His hope was evaporating again, just as it had so many times in the past.

'He told me everything. I know what he said to you that made you leave.'

Sam closed his eyes, put his chin on her shoulder and let the world pass them by. It was a rude, coarse and unkind place—all the things that their love was not. But perhaps it suited him. Her father was right in one thing: he was unworthy of such a woman. 'I am sorry,' he said.

'You needn't be. I am sorry. I was the one who doubted. But never again.' She nestled against his chest and he imagined what it would be like, when they had exhausted themselves making love, to sleep with her just like this.

'Never again,' he agreed. 'My darling Evelyn.'

She lifted her head and kissed him on the corner of the mouth. 'And you may call me Evie, again, by the way. Or Evelyn. Or Eve. Anything you like, really.'

Anything I like. These swooping highs and lows of emotion could not be good for his blood pressure. But the possibilities in the word *anything* made him dizzy. 'More than anything, I think I should like to call you Mrs Hastings,' he said and waited for her to contradict him.

'I should like that as well.' She smiled and kissed him again, tugging his arm to move him towards the carriage. 'Perhaps we could get the special licence from Michael. Then we might be married tomorrow.'

'Not without your father's consent,' he reminded her. 'You have another month until you are of age.' When Thorne learned of their plans, there would be hell to pay. But it would be worth the price.

'I do not mean to wait that long,' she said.

'Neither do I.' He imagined the deep cushions and well-upholstered squabs that waited, just behind the carriage door.

'We will have to go to Scotland. But not Gretna Green. You must show me Edinburgh.'

It was a very long ride to Edinburgh. Several days. And the whole of it would be spent alone with Evie. Perhaps brother Michael did not mean to be so generous with his equipage as that. But the matter could be settled when they returned.

'Oh, Lady Evelyn, I think you are right,' he said, taking control and pulling her after him, up into the carriage, and into his lap. He imagined what would happen when his Evie met his teachers, his colleagues and perhaps his students. 'I must show you Edinburgh. And we shall see what it makes of you.' He grinned. It would be far more dangerous than going to sea. But it would never be dull.

* * * * *